传媒英语热点阅读
Hot Issues in the News

（第 3 册）

主　编　林俊伟

副主编　韩　莉　杨　雯

编　委　李　婷　郭　玮　刘　航　郭艳萍

　　　　　柳婷婷　周　妍　王连芬　韩　莉

　　　　　杨　雯　林俊伟

东南大学出版社

·南京·

图书在版编目（CIP）数据

传媒英语热点阅读. 第 3 册/林俊伟主编. —南京：
东南大学出版社,2010.8
ISBN　978 - 7 - 5641 - 2358 - 1

Ⅰ.①传…　Ⅱ.①林…　Ⅲ.①传播媒介—英语
—阅读教学—自学参考资料　Ⅳ.①H319.4

中国版本图书馆 CIP 数据核字(2010)第 148386 号

传媒英语热点阅读（第 3 册）

主　编	林俊伟	责任编辑	刘　坚	
电　话	(025)83793329/83362442(传真)	电子邮件	liu-jian@ seu. edu. cn	
出版发行	东南大学出版社	出 版 人	江　汉	
地　址	南京市四牌楼 2 号(210096)	邮　编	210096	
销售电话	(025)83792327/83794561/83794174/83794121/			
	83795802/57711295(传真)			
网　址	http://www. seupress. com	电子邮件	press@ seu. edu. cn	
经　销	全国各地新华书店	印　刷	南京新洲印刷有限公司	
开　本	718mm×1005mm　1/16	印　张	12.75	字　数　290 千字
印　数	1—4500 册			
版　次	2010 年 8 月第 1 版　2010 年 8 月第 1 次印刷			
书　号	ISBN　978 - 7 - 5641 - 2358 - 1			
定　价	23.00 元			

PREFACE 前言

　　传媒英语（Media English）为专门用途英语（English for Specific Purpose）的一种，其主要功能是通过不同主题的选材，为读者的多元观点和思考空间提供元素，并借此加深学习者对于新闻传媒专业的理解，提高他们运用专业语言的能力。在全球化的大趋势下，具备良好的专业英语素质显然是一个具有国际视野、有开拓性和前瞻性的传媒从业人员的必备前提。

　　本书共四册，主要面向传媒院校学生、传媒从业人员、从事跨国贸易或其他具有与国外交流行业背景的人员。编者们力图使本书具备下列特色：

　　1. 创新教材编写思路。编者们拟尽其所能将每年 7 月 1 日至 12 月 31 日间由全球主流传媒机构报道或评论的世界热点话题加以理性选择，分门别类，编辑成第二、第四册，供春季学期使用；将每年 1 月 1 日至 6 月 30 日的热点话题编辑成第一、第三册，供秋季学期使用。每年修订一版，与时俱进。

　　2. 提供全球视野。编者们以为培养英语学习者的跨文化意识以及全球视野比传授语言知识更重要。井底之蛙，恐成夜郎自大笑柄。本书每册含有 10 个单元，每单元有 3 篇文章，从不同视角谈论相关话题，见仁见智。文章主要出自英、美两国，亚洲、非洲和南美洲的主流媒体。本册关注的话题主要是：冰岛火山喷发，欧债危机，墨西哥湾漏油事件，南非世界杯，日本政坛风云，世界经济复苏，火星计划等。

　　3. 习得时代英语。编者们相信媒体的语言最能体现时代特色，也具有时代文化符号意义。编者们希望与本书有缘的人能耐心地阅读喜欢的文章，积累热点词汇，一鸣惊人。

　　本书的十位编者都是中国传媒大学南广学院公共英语教学部的教师。除了主编人到中年，才疏学浅外，其余九位都是朝气蓬勃、激情四射、好学上进的年轻潮人。书中如有冒犯之举，皆非编者们的主观行为。如能得到你的谅解，我们不胜感激，否则，一切责任皆由本书主编一人承担。

　　参加本书编写的主要还有：直长亮、薛棋文、赖敏、孟雅、秦智娟、李涛、杨青、罗金妮、张云、李璐、郑小彗、王涛涛、刘艳青，李婷等。

　　感谢东南大学出版社的英美文学博士刘坚先生。他的热情和细心使得本书得以顺利出版。

林俊伟

于中国传媒大学南广学院

2010 年 7 月

Contents

Unit One

Arts and Culture

 Section A

"Hubble Bubble" Tower Will Be Icon of Olympic Legacy

(ARUP) The ArcelorMittal Orbit will have a viewing platform and restaurant at the top

The Issue in the News

As is known to all, the 2012 Summer Olympic Games are scheduled to take place in London, United Kingdom, from 27 July to 12 August 2012. The Olympics prompted a redevelopment of many of the areas of London in which the games are to be held. And in order to meet the Olympic Games, Britain will invest much money in building a red tower that looks like a mangled rollercoaster as the new icon of the city London and the Olympic Park. Turner Prize-winning artist Anish Kapoor is the designer of this tower. He unveiled his design for the £19million sculpture recently. Lakshmi Mittal, the steel magnate who is the fifth richest man in the world will supply much of the 1,400 tons of steel for this looping, deep red-coloured tower.

Points to Notice

As you read, pay attention to the following facets and information mentioned in this piece of news:

- Anish Kapoor—the designer of this tower
- Tessa Jowell—The Olympics Minister
- the name of this tower
- Lakshmi Mittal—the backer of this project

Text

By Ben Hoyle, Arts Correspondent

April 1, 2010

More than 120 years after Gustave Eiffel[1] built the steel lattice that came to symbolise Paris, London is taking on the City of Light with the Colossus of Stratford—at least, that is one of the names the capital's mayor has in mind.

The Olympics Minister Tessa Jowell sees Anish Kapoor's work as a way of making the site of the 2012 Games stand out. East London will have the largest and most ambitious artwork in the country: a startling red tower that looks like a mangled rollercoaster.

It is too early to tell what the world will call this £19.1 million, 115m-tall (377ft) feat of technological and industrial wizardry, but another of the mayor Boris Johnson's favourite titles is The Hubble-Bubble.

Kapoor beat competition from the artist Antony Gormley and the architects

Caruso St John to win the mayor's contest to find yet another "iconic symbol" for the city and the Olympic Park. Detailed plans were revealed yesterday at the Greater London Assembly headquarters.

Officially the structure, which will be 22m taller than the Statue of Liberty and more than twice the height of Nelson's Column, is called the ArcelorMittal Orbit[2]. It is named after the steel company owned by Lakshmi Mittal[3], the richest man in Britain, who is paying most of the cost—and planting a giant advert in the Olympic site. However Mr Johnson immediately bombarded his new landmark with a fusillade of alternative names.

"Some may choose to think of it as the Colossus of Stratford," he said. "Some eyes may detect a helter-skelter or a supersized mutant trombone. Some may even see the world's biggest ever representation of a shisha pipe and call it The Hubble-Bubble. But I know that it is the ArcelorMittal Orbit. It represents the dynamism of a city coming out of recession and the embodiment of the cross-fertilisation of cultures and styles that makes London the world capital of arts, the cultural and creative industries."

Whatever it ends up being called, the Orbit is the latest and priciest example of a vogue for gargantuan public art commissions, begun by Gormley's Angel of the North in 1998 and continuing now with Mark Wallinger's planned 50m tall horse near the Eurostar terminal at Ebbsfleet in Kent. Mr Johnson said that £ 3.1 million of the cost would be borne by the Greater London Authority[4], with Mr Mittal picking up the rest. "I know very well that there will be people who say we are nuts, we are barmy in the depths of a recession to be building Britain's biggest ever piece of public art," he said.

However, although the Olympics area already had the stadium, the aquatics centre and a giant shopping mall, he and Ms Jowell had long felt that "we needed to give that site something extra, something to distinguish the East London skyline, something to arouse the curiosity and wonder of Londoners and visitors alike". They needed money to make it possible, and steel, so Mr Johnson was overjoyed to find himself sharing a cloakroom with Mr Mittal at Davos in

January 2009.

The meeting lasted 45 seconds. Mr Mittal said that Mr Johnson spoke for all of them but by the end of it they had a deal. The Mayor rebutted suggestions that the structure would be an improper incursion of corporate branding into public life, pointing out that Olympics rules meant it could not carry the company name during the Games.

Mr Kapoor said he wanted to take on the Eiffel Tower and the memory of the "birdsnest stadium" from the last Olympics by trying to "rethink" the idea of a tower. Lifts and a walkway will enable 800 people an hour to get to the top, where there will be a restaurant and viewing platform.

http://www. timesonline. co. uk/tol/news/uk/article7083022. ece

Online Resources

http://www. thisislondon. co. uk/standard/article-23820823-boris-johnsons-2012-tower-is-a-real-eyeful. do

http://www. tingclass. com/article/0023299574369. html

http://cyberboris. wordpress. com/2010/03/31/hubble-bubble-from-anish-kapoor/

Vocabulary

1.	lattice	n.	framework consisting of an ornamental design made of strips of wood or metal
2.	mangle	vt.	alter so as to make unrecognizable
3.	rollercoaster	n.	elevated railway in an amusement park (usually with sharp curves and steep inclines)
4.	wizardry	n.	exceptional creative ability
5.	bombard	vt.	address with continuously or persistently, as if with a barrage
6.	fusillade	n.	rapid simultaneous discharge of firearms
7.	dynamism	n.	active strength of body or mind
8.	embodiment	n.	a new personification of a familiar idea

9. gargantuan   *adj.* of great mass; huge and bulky

10. barmy   *adj.* informal or slang terms for mentally irregular

11. aquatic   *n.* sports that involve bodies of water

12. incursion   *n.* the act of entering some territory or domain (often in large numbers)

13. rebut   *vt.* overthrow by argument, evidence, or proof

Language Notes

1. Alexandre Gustave **Eiffel** né Bönickhausen (December 15, 1832—December 27, 1923): French structural engineer from the École Centrale Paris, an entrepreneur and a specialist of metallic structures. He is famous for designing the Eiffel Tower, built 1887—1889 for the 1889 Universal Exposition in Paris, France, the armature for the Statue of Liberty, New York Harbor, United States and the San Sebastian Church in Manila, Philippines.

2. **The ArcelorMittal Orbit**: a 115 metres (377 ft) high observation tower planned for the Olympic Park in Stratford, London. The steel sculpture will be Britain's largest piece of public art, and is intended to be a permanent, lasting legacy of London's hosting of the 2012 Summer Olympics, assisting in the post-Olympics regeneration of the Stratford area. Sited between the Olympic Stadium and the Aquatics Centre, it will allow visitors to view the whole Olympic Park from two observation platforms.

3. **Lakshmi Niwas Mittal**: an Indian steel tycoon, philanthropist, and the chairman and chief executive officer of ArcelorMittal. As of July 2010, Mittal is the richest man in Europe and the fifth richest in the world with a personal wealth of US $ 28.7 billion or £ 19.3 billion. The Financial Times named Mittal Person of the Year in 2006. In May 2007, he was named one of the "100 Most Influential People" by Time magazine.

4. **The Greater London Authority** (GLA): the top-tier administrative body for Greater London, UK. It consists of a directly-elected executive Mayor of London, currently Boris Johnson, and an elected 25-member London Assembly

with scrutiny powers. The authority was established in 2000, following a local referendum, and derives most of its powers from the Greater London Authority Act 1999 and the Greater London Authority Act 2007.

Exercises

 Vocabulary and Expressions

A. Idioms and Expressions

Fill in the blanks with the correct idiom or expression.

1. have in mind: intend to refer to 考虑到,打算

Just tell us the color and design you have in mind. we'll change them accordingly.

2. be nuts about 狂热于

She's beautiful. I'm nuts about her.

3. take on: admit into a group or community 呈现,穿上

The lizard can take on the colors of its background.

1. Camping in summer is just what I _____.

2. The old factory _____ a new look.

3. This would allow foreigners to learn about our gourmet offerings before they could appreciate and _____ them.

B. Vocabulary

Fill in the blanks with the words given below. Change the form where necessary.

rebut wizardry embodiment dynamism aquatic
bombard incursion gargantuan mangle rollercoaster

1. Employment is the direct _____ of the citizens' right to work.

2. My _____, pristine machine was good for writing papers and playing solitaire, and that was all.

3. It takes more than high-tech _____ to capture deep-ocean creatures on film.

4. He attempts to _____ the assertion made by the prosecution witness.

5. He was off work because he'd _____ his hand in a machine.

6. Enemy forces have made _____ into our territory.

7. The new journal is _____ with letters of criticism from the subscribers.

8. _____ sports include swimming and rowing.

9. Shanghai is an international metropolis full of vigor, _____ and variety.

10. Going on a _____ was a big thrill for everyone.

✉ Exploring Content

A. Read the following statements, and then mark T(True) if the statement agrees with the information given in the passage, mark F(False) if the statement contradicts the information given in the passage.

1. The Olympics Minister Tessa Jowell sees Anish Kapoor's work as a way of making the site of the 2012 Games stand out.

2. Kapoor beat competition from the artist Gustave Eiffel and the architects Lakshmi Mittal to win the mayor's contest to find yet another "iconic symbol" for the city and the Olympic Park.

3. Some may even see the world's biggest ever representation of a shisha pipe and call it The Hubble-Bubble.

4. The Colossus of Stratford represents the dynamism of a city coming out of recession and the embodiment of the cross-fertilisation of cultures and styles that makes London the world capital of arts, the cultural and creative industries.

5. Mr. Kapoor said he wanted to take on the Eiffel Tower and the memory of the "birdsnest stadium" from the Sydney Olympics by trying to "rethink" the idea of a tower.

B. Find the synonym in the reading.

1. Find a word in Paragraph 1 that means **stand for or represent**.
   _____

2. Find a word in Paragraph 2 that means **surprising**.
   _____

3. Find a word in Paragraph 4 that means **unveil or display**.
   _____

4. Find a word in Paragraph 7 that means *trend or style*. _____

5. Find a word in Paragraph 8 that means *jumbo or huge*. _____

✉ Translation

Translate the following sentences into Chinese.

1. East London will have the largest and most ambitious artwork in the country: a startling red tower that looks like a mangled rollercoaster.

2. Mr Johnson said that £ 3. 1 million of the cost would be borne by the Greater London Authority, with Mr Mittal picking up the rest.

3. "I know very well that there will be people who say we are nuts, we are barmy in the depths of a recession to be building Britain's biggest ever piece of public art," he said.

4. It is named after the steel company owned by Lakshmi Mittal, the richest man in Britain, who is paying most of the cost.

5. Lifts and a walkway will enable 800 people an hour to get to the top, where there will be a restaurant and viewing platform.

✉ Cloze

Complete the following short passage by choosing proper words from the word bank provided.

monument structure offered satisfy unveiled instantly described
previous viewing terribly twist entire competition collision proper

It looks like a catastrophic __1__ between two cranes on the Olympic site. But this towering, twisted mass of metal will be Britain's lasting __2__ to the nation's role in hosting the 2012 games. Turner Prize-winning artist Anish Kapoor __3__ his design for the £ 19million sculpture yesterday, a ruby red, helter skelter-style structure that, at 377ft, will stand more than twice as tall as Nelson's column. It was __4__ nicknamed the Eyeful Tower and likened enthusiastically by London Mayor Boris Johnson to a giant "hubble-bubble" shisha pipe. But contributors to Twitter and similar internet sites took only minutes to criticise the work. One __5__ it as "a rollercoaster that costs £ 19million a go". Other early phrases included "twisted spaghetti", "horrific squiggles" and "Meccano on crack". Work on the officially-named ArcelorMittal Orbit, which will house a restaurant and __6__ platform, has yet to start and it still needs planning permission. About 700 visitors an hour will be able to visit the site next to the 193 feet high Olympic stadium. The tower will have a viewing platform and an outdoor walkway. At its unveiling today, Kapoor, 56, said it was "thrilling" to be __7__ the chance to create for the capital something on a par with what Gustave Eiffel made in Paris "It would be __8__ arrogant to compete with Eiffel who spent his __9__ life making that thing," said Kapoor. "What we're trying to make is the best thing we can do". The artist sees his looping, deep red-coloured tower as "an eccentric __10__ that looks as if it's going to fall over".

Discussion

Discuss the following questions with your class.

1. Could you list the icons of famous cities like Shanghai, New York, and Tokyo?
2. In your opinion, what is the most impressive event in 2008 Olympics?
3. If you were a designer, what kind of landmark would you design for London?
4. What occurs to you when someone mentions "London" or "Britain"?

Section B

Channel 4 Gives *Romeo and Juliet* a Twitter Twist

31 March 2010

Romeo and Juliet is to be "tweeted" in a link up between Channel 4 and the Royal Shakespeare Company (RSC) as part of the broadcaster's new arts line-up.

Such Tweet Sorrow will tell the story of the Shakespearian tragedy via the social networking website Twitter.

Channel 4 has vowed to double its arts programmes commissioning budget on its core channel to £ 6m every year.

The broadcaster also announced it had appointed More4 editor Tabitha Jackson as its new arts commissioning editor.

Such Tweet Sorrow will go live on 12 April, but exact details are being kept under wraps until nearer the time.

Classical music

Channel 4's beefed up arts portfolio will also include a prime time series following the Halle Orchestra as it builds a new orchestra of young musicians.

The orchestra will demonstrate the "transformative" power that classical music can have on young people.

"Landmark" series Young, Autistic And Stagestruck will follow nine autistic children from across the UK who come together to produce their own musical show.

Channel 4 director of television and content Kevin Lygo said: "Channel 4 will continue to seek a distinctive approach to its arts coverage, focusing most of our activity on the vibrant contemporary arts scene in Britain today and the visual arts in particular.

"We want to position ourselves as both an aggregator and instigator of the most interesting and challenging art work going on across Britain today. "

It was also revealed that digital channel More4 has forged a partnership with Arts Council England working with major artists and institutions to celebrate British contemporary art.

The first product of the partnership, The Royal Ballet in Cuba, made by the Ballet Boyz, will be broadcast at Christmas.

Forthcoming More4 films include a six-part series featuring leading arts figures such as film director Martin Scorsese, artist David Hockney and singer Jessye Norman as they mentor a young person for a year.

The channel will also feature a documentary based on the life of playwright Andrea Dunbar, who wrote the film Rita, Sue And Bob Too.

Film4, is also said to be in the "early development stage" on new films with prominent British artists including the Chapman Brothers.

http://news.bbc.co.uk/2/hi/entertainment/arts_and_culture/8597734.stm

Vocabulary

Match each word to its definition.

1. portfolio	(	) a.	a musical organization consisting of a group of instrumentalists including string players
2. orchestra	(	) b.	vigorous and active
3. vibrant	(	) c.	serve as a teacher or trusted counselor
4. forge	(	) d.	a set of pieces of creative work collected to be shown to potential customers or employers
5. mentor	(	) e.	having a quality that thrusts itself into attention

6. prominent   (   ) f. available when required or as promised

7. forthcoming   (   ) g. come up with (an idea, plan, explanation, theory, or principle) after a mental effort;

Discussion

Discuss the following questions with your class.

1. What do you know about Shakespeare? Could you list some of his famous works?

2. What is Twitter? Do you have your own blog?

3. Do you know the story *Romeo and Juliet*? If yes, introduce this play to your classmates.

4. If you were a director, how would you improve audience rating?

■ Section C ■

The Post Wins Four Pulitzers; Bristol, Va., Paper Wins for Public Service

By Howard Kurtz

April 13, 2010

The Washington Post won four Pulitzer Prizes on Monday for reporting on subjects ranging from war to modern dance, and the New York Times won three awards, including one shared with ProPublica, a new nonprofit organization created to pursue investigative journalism.

The public service medal went to a small Virginia newspaper, the Bristol Herald Courier, for examining the state's mismanagement of natural-gas royalties.

Among The Post's winners, Gene Weingarten, who received the feature writing award for his story on parents who accidentally killed their children by leaving them in cars, said he came close to doing the same thing with his daughter 25 years ago. Anthony Shadid won the international reporting prize for a series on the Iraq war.

Sarah Kaufman, who writes about dance and movement in venues as wide-ranging as movies and viral videos, took the criticism award. Kathleen Parker, whose columns are syndicated by the Washington Post Writers Group, won the Pulitzer for commentary.

David E. Hoffman, a former Washington Post assistant managing editor for foreign news, won a Pulitzer in the general nonfiction category for "The Dead Hand: The Untold Story of the Cold War Arms Race and Its Dangerous Legacy." The board's citation called the book "a well documented narrative that examines the terrifying doomsday competition between two superpowers and how weapons of mass destruction still imperil humankind."

The National Enquirer, which drew attention by entering its exposé of John Edwards fathering a child with a former presidential campaign aide, was not a finalist. The prizes are administered by Columbia University.

ProPublica, which launched just more than two years ago, employs 35 journalists and has teamed with major newspapers and networks, is the first independent nonprofit organization to win a Pulitzer. "The prizes are nice, but what's really nice is that it suggests our nonprofit, nonpartisan model can work," said founding editor Paul Steiger.

ProPublica's Sheri Fink shared the investigative reporting prize with the New York Times Magazine for reporting on decisions made by exhausted doctors whose hospital was cut off by Hurricane Katrina. The Pulitzer board awarded a second investigative prize to Barbara Laker and Wendy Ruderman of the Philadelphia Daily News for exposing a rogue police narcotics squad.

Weingarten, whose Pulitzer was his second, called his examination of child deaths "the hardest story I've ever done... There was nothing in it for these people to talk to me, except the chance to save a life." He said that a quarter-century ago he almost left his toddler in the back seat when he forgot to drop her at day care, until she spoke as he was leaving the car.

"It's a shame you carry with you forever... My heart kept leaping into my mouth with recognition of what had almost happened," Weingarten said. He said that when he told his daughter Molly, now 28, "I couldn't look her in the eye."

Kaufman, who studied ballet at a Bethesda academy as a young woman, said her work was first published in college after she called the Washington City Paper and complained that it ran no dance reviews. "To the extent I can capture my experience in the theater and bring the reader there with me, it's a joy to be able to do that," she said.

Part of her job, Kaufman said, is "to say in a beautiful way what's obvious about an art form." But particularly in dance, she said, "there's not enough scholarship, there's not enough rigorous journalism that asks hard questions... I've always viewed myself as a journalist, as a reporter first."

Parker said that when she left her South Carolina home six years ago with a U-Haul trailer to rent a studio apartment in Washington, "nobody had ever heard of me"—despite the fact that she was widely syndicated. "There's this idea you don't exist unless you're in Washington... When you say something on the pages of The Washington Post, it's just different."

Parker, whose column started appearing regularly on the Post op-ed page 18 months ago, began her career as a one-woman bureau in Palatka, Fla., and still commutes to the South Carolina home she shares with her husband. "Basically, I'm in a bunker, writing what I think," she said. "I have never tried to please anyone. I have never thought about what the reader would think, and that's very easy when you're alone." Her winning columns included pieces on national politics, abortion and her childhood love of Nancy Drew.

Widely viewed as right-leaning, Parker received 12,000 hostile e-mails after writing in National Review Online that Sarah Palin was unqualified to be vice president. But Parker resists the label, saying, "Sometimes I'm conservative; sometimes I'm not."

Shadid, a former Baghdad bureau chief who also won his second Pulitzer, spoke from Boston, two days after his wife had a baby. He returned to Iraq after a two-year absence "to write against the narrative that the war was over," Shadid said. "There was a sense in the public that there was an invasion and an occupation, that it turned out okay, and it was a lot more complicated than that."

What he tried to examine, said Shadid, who joined the New York Times earlier this year, is "what did America leave behind—what kind of society, what kind of government, what kind of landscape?"

Daniel Gilbert, one of the seven reporters at the Bristol paper, near the Tennessee border, answered the phone when a Post reporter called the newsroom. "It's a rush, for sure," he said of the prize.

Gilbert said the natural-gas investigation "took 13 months of reporting incrementally, a little bit every week, every month."

Matt Richtel and the New York Times staff won the national reporting award for their work on distracted driving caused by cellphones and other devices. Michael Moss and the Times staff received the explanatory reporting prize for work on food safety issues.

The local reporting prize went to Raquel Rutledge of the Milwaukee Journal Sentinel for stories on fraud and abuse in a child-care program. The Seattle Times won the breaking-news award for its coverage, both in print and online, of the shooting deaths of four police officers and the 40-hour manhunt that followed.

Three Dallas Morning News staff writers—Tod Robberson, Colleen McCain Nelson and William McKenzie—won the Pulitzer for editorial writing. Mary Chind of the Des Moines Register captured the prize for breaking news photography for a daring rescue near a broken dam, and Craig Walker of the Denver Post won for feature photography.

The editorial cartooning prize went to Mark Fiore, who syndicates himself and appears on the San Francisco Chronicle site, SFGate. com.

http://www. washingtonpost. com/wp-dyn/content/article/2010/04/12/ AR2010041202071. html? hpid% 3Dtopnews

Discussion

Discuss the following questions with your class.

1. What do you know about Pulitzer Prize?

2. Do you think prize can encourage artists to create outstanding works?

3. What is a journalist's first duty when confronting disaster, reporting or saving victims?

4. Do you think photos play an important role in news reporting? Why or why not?

Unit Two

Entertainment and Trends

Section A

Designer Has Fan at Top, but Too Few at the Stores

The Issue in the News

Michelle Obama, the First Lady of the United States, the corporate lawyer with a big education, is good at tempering her own strong personality with d modernized version of another era's ladylike clothes. One of her favorite designers is Maria Pinto, but she has closed the doors of her once-popular Chicago shop and filed for bankruptcy protection recently. Pinto started her own label in 1991, but really hit her stride in 2008 when her dresses were showcased by rising star Obama in an array of glossy women's magazine spreads and high-profile TV appearances. Pinto's prices ranged from $ 350 to upwards of $ 5,000—failed to truly reach a national stage and her clientele remained largely limited to Chicago's elite. High price in the current economic climate is the reason why Pinto's celeb-favored fashion house had to shutter its doors.

Points to Notice

As you read, pay attention to the following facets and information mentioned in this piece of news:

● Michelle Obama—the first lady of the United States

● Maria Pinto—a 53 years old designer

● Mrs-O. org—a blog devoted to Mrs. Obama's clothes.

● The reason why Ms. Pinto abruptly put up a "closeout sale" sign in the window of her boutique

Text

April 30, 2010

CHICAGO—Fashion and politics are seasonal and unpredictable, yet the two came together quite well here for the hometown designer Maria Pinto and Michelle Obama[1], whose first memorable bursts onto the national scene were often in Pinto creations.

Remember the purple sheath Mrs. Obama wore the night of the fist bump heard round the world? The teal number at the Democratic National Convention[2]? Or the red dress she wore to meet the Bushes on their way out of the White House? Maria Pinto[3] all, designed right here where both women were born and raised and, over the course of one remarkable election, became stars.

So when Ms. Pinto abruptly put up a "closeout sale" sign in the window of her West Loop boutique and announced that she was folding her fashion business, Chicago—and Pinto devotees all over—reacted with disbelief: What in sartorial heaven happened? "I pushed as far as I could," Ms. Pinto, 53, said in her first lengthy interview since the demise of her store and wholesale operations in mid-February.

Just back from a month's break in Barcelona, she pointed to the strain that a sour economy had placed on her business just as it was expanding and gaining major traction beyond a loyal Chicago following.

But Ms. Pinto acknowledged having made some typical startup mistakes in building her brand, in areas like financial management and operations.

After 16 years of designing out of a somewhat anonymous atelier, she opened the boutique, named after herself, in August 2008, capitalizing on a wave of enthusiasm for her work, as displayed mostly by Mrs. Obama on the campaign trail. She also increased her wholesale operations and had been maintaining a showroom in New York.

While Mrs. Obama diversified her style after becoming first lady (she has been drawn to high-end designers like Jason Wu[4] and Narciso Rodriguez[5], as well as brands like J. Crew), she still sported Maria Pinto every now and then. But even high-profile support of the brand, priced in the hundreds and thousands of dollars, could not save it from the reality of the Great Recession.

The real problems started right after the introduction of the spring 2010 line in New York last September, Ms. Pinto said. "They loved the line," she said. "I was like, where are the orders? O. K. , this is not a good sign."

Pinto was carried at stores like Barneys, Saks Fifth Avenue and Takashimaya—a store whose New York location will soon be closing its doors, another victim of the recession.

"She's such a highly regarded talent," said Anne Brouwer of McMillan Doolittle, a Chicago firm that specializes in retail analysis. "It was certainly a really difficult time to open."

Still, fashion watchers said her style helped define a moment. "As a fan of the first lady's, I was discovering Michelle Obama's style influence, and Maria Pinto was part of that story from the very beginning," said Mary Tomer, creator of Mrs-O. org, a blog devoted to Mrs. Obama's clothes.

But Mrs. Obama chose from the conservative end of Ms. Pinto's collections, which also included pieces like leather jeans, dresses of sassy feathers and kangaroo jackets. There is so much more the designer wishes she could have been known for.

"Yes, it was heartbreaking and very sad," Ms. Pinto said of the last few months. "The good news is that my creativity goes with me anywhere I go."

For now, it will go into yoga, gardening, painting—and a lot of soul-searching.

http://www. nytimes. com/2010/05/01/us/politics/01maria. html? ref = style

Online Resources

http://njuice. com/gslqb-Dressing-Obama-Success-Then-Going-Business-NYTimescom

http://news. style. com/story/comments/designer _ has _ fan _ at _ top _ but _ too _ few _ at _ the _ stores _ new _ york _ times/748127/

http://twitter. com/womenandbiz/status/15490574816

Vocabulary

1.	sheath	n.	a dress suitable for formal occasions
2.	abruptly	adv.	quickly and without warning
3.	sartorial	adj.	of or relating to a tailor or to tailoring
4.	boutique	n.	a shop that sells women's clothes and jewelry
5.	lengthy	adj.	relatively long in duration; tediously protracted
6.	demise	n.	the time when something ends
7.	strain	n.	difficulty that causes worry or emotional tension
8.	traction	n.	the friction between a body and the surface on which it moves (as between an automobile tire and the road)
9.	startup	n.	the act of starting a new operation or practice
10.	atelier	n.	a studio especially for an artist or designer

23

Language Notes

1. **Michelle LaVaughn Robinson Obama** (born January 17, 1964): wife of the President of the United States, Barack Obama, and is the First Lady of the United States. Michelle Robinson was born in and grew up on the South Side of Chicago. She received her bachelor's degree from Princeton University and her Juris Doctor (J. D.) from Harvard Law School. After completing her formal education, she returned to Chicago and accepted a position with the law firm Sidley Austin, where she met her future husband. Subsequently, she worked as part of the staff of Chicago mayor Richard M. Daley, and for the University of Chicago Medical Center. Throughout 2007 and 2008, she helped campaign for her husband's presidential bid and delivered a keynote address at the 2008 Democratic National Convention. She is the mother of two daughters, Malia and Sasha, and is the sister of Craig Robinson, men's basketball coach at Oregon State University.

2. The **Democratic National Convention**: a series of presidential nominating conventions held every four years since 1832 by the United States Democratic Party. [1] They have been administered by the Democratic National Committee since the 1852 national convention. The primary goal of the Democratic National Convention is to nominate and confirm a candidate for President and Vice President, adopt a comprehensive party platform and unify the party.

3. **Maria Pinto**: the woman behind Michelle Obama's dresses. She is a fashion designer who became famous after the First Lady wore her designs but sadly, according to recent reports, she will close her company.

4. **Jason Wu** (traditional Chinese: 吴季刚) (born September 27, 1982, a Manhattan-based American fashion designer. Born in Taiwan, Wu moved to Vancouver, British Columbia, Canada at age nine and attended Eaglebrook School in Deerfield, Massachusetts and Loomis Chaffee, in Connecticut. He learned how to sew by designing and sewing for dolls, and went on to study sculpture in Tokyo. Wu continued this career path at sixteen by learning to

create freelance doll clothing designs for toy company Integrity. Michelle Obama was introduced to Wu by André Leon Talley, Vogue Magazine's editor-at-large, who had been advising the future First Family on their appearance.

5. Narciso Rodriguez III (born 27 January 1961): an American fashion designer. In 2005, he became the first American to win the Council of Fashion Designers of America Womenswear Designer of the Year Award two years in a row. On November 4, 2008, Michelle Obama wore a dress from Narciso Rodriguez's spring 2009 collection when she joined her husband, Barack Obama, appearing for the first time as president-elect of the United States, on the stage at Grant Park in Chicago;

Exercises

 Vocabulary and Expressions

A. Idioms and Expressions

Fill in the blanks with the correct idiom or expression.

1. specialize in 专攻,专门从事于(某一科目)

In fact, we specialize in this with a long history.

2. name after 以……的名字起名

The child was named after its father, given its father's first name.

3. devote to 把……专用于,完全用于(某事或做某事);致力于……

He has been devoting his whole life to benefiting mankind.

1. They _____ the new-born dog _____ his dead grandfather.

2. I _____ the sale of cotton piece goods. May I act as your agent?

3. The newspaper _____ two pages _____ comics.

B. Vocabulary

Fill in the blanks with the words given below. Change the form where necessary.

| abrupt | startup | strain | boutique | demise | traction | sartorial | lengthy |

1. He was breaking up under the _____.

2. About 20 Chinatown garment workers—who said their boss _____ closed up shop, leaving them high and dry at Christmas—yesterday demanded $40,000 in back pay.

3. He praised the union's aims but predicted its early _____.

4. The _____ of the new factory was delayed by strikes.

5. John has never been known for his _____ elegance.

6. The professor wrote a _____ book on Napoleon.

7. I've had a look at the dresses in the new _____, but they're nothing to write home about.

8. We may continue the _____ up to three weeks, until the fracture is healed.

Exploring Content

A. Complete the sentences based on the reading text.

1. Maria Pinto all, designed right here _____ and, over the course of one remarkable election, became stars.

2. But Ms. Pinto acknowledged having made some typical startup mistakes in building her brand, in areas like _____.

3. While Mrs. Obama diversified her style after becoming first lady, _____ _____.

4. Pinto was carried at stores like Barneys, Saks Fifth Avenue and Takashimaya—a store _____, another victim of the recession.

5. As a fan of the first lady's, _____, and Maria Pinto was part of that story from the very beginning.

B. Put a check(✓) next to the statements that the writer would agree with.

1. ( ) Fashion and politics are seasonal and unpredictable, yet the two came together quite well here for the hometown designer Narciso Rodriguez and

Michelle Obama, whose first memorable bursts onto the national scene were often in Pinto creations.

2. (   ) Just back from a month's break in Barcelona, Ms. Pinto pointed to the strain that a sour economy had placed on her business just as it was expanding and gaining major traction beyond a loyal Chicago following.

3. (   ) Ms. Pinto also increased her wholesale operations and had been maintaining a showroom in Washington.

4. (   ) Mrs. Obama chose from the conservative end of Ms. Pinto's collections, which also included pieces like leather jeans, dresses of sassy feathers and kangaroo jackets.

5. (   ) Ms. Pinto said of the last few months, "The good news is that my creativity goes with me anywhere I go. "

✉ Translation

Translate the following sentences into Chinese.

1. Fashion and politics are seasonal and unpredictable.

2. Ms. Pinto acknowledged having made some typical startup mistakes in building her brand, in areas like financial management and operations.

3. Mrs. Obama diversified her style after becoming first lady.

4. Even (Mrs. Obama's) high-profile support of the brand, priced in the hundreds and thousands of dollars, could not save it from the reality of the Great Recession.

5. "Yes, it was heartbreaking and very sad, " Ms. Pinto said of the last few months. "The good news is that my creativity goes with me anywhere I go. "

✉ Cloze

Complete the following short passage by choosing proper words from the word bank provided.

reality	choice	discovered	favorite	appear	election	wore	craft
define	creative	addict	earnings	editor	interviewed	depressed	

Jason Wu made fashion history when First Lady Michelle Obama chose his one-of-a-kind floor length white chiffon gown for the Presidential Inaugural balls on January 20, 2009. At just 26 years of age, Mrs. Obama's __1__ put him at the epicenter of the fashion media world. Looking back at his remarkable rise, we found that many Hollywood celebrities had __2__ Jason Wu long before Inauguration night.

Jason Wu was born in Taiwan, and learned his __3__ at a young age by designing and sewing clothing for dolls. At 16 he started freelance designing doll clothing for a toy company. By 17 he was named __4__ director of Integrity Toys. After studying at Parsons, he landed an internship with Narciso Rodriguez, another one of the First Lady's __5__ designers.

With __6__ from his doll designs, Jason Wu was able to debut his first full collection in 2006. Many of Jason's early clients __7__ in the photo gallery above. According to reports, a Vogue magazine __8__ introduced Michelle to Jason's work. Last November she __9__ a Jason Wu dress while being __10__ by Barbara Walters.

Discussion

Discuss the following questions with your class.

1. How do you define fashion?
2. Do you think a celebrity's support can help a brand earn its reputation?
3. In your opinion, what factors contribute to a brand's success?
4. What do you know about Mrs. Obama?

■ **Section B** ■

Celebrity Rehab Uncovered

By Peter Bowes

30 April 2010

It is rare for a week to go by without news of a celebrity or sports star checking themselves into a rehabilitation centre.

Britney Spears, Lindsay Lohan and Tiger Woods have all had their problems.

Whether it is alcohol, drugs or an uncontrollable compulsion to have sex, the addictions of high-profile people attract headlines and a level of treatment few others can afford.

Such is the fascination with showbiz stars and their issues that VH1's Celebrity Rehab has become a big hit.

The show, which features celebrities as they undergo treatment, has reportedly offered Lohan $ 1m (£ 652,000) to appear on its next series.

But most celebrities prefer to deal with their problems in private. Many check in to the Promises Treatment Centre in Malibu which offers residential treatment for the well-heeled.

Nestled in the hills above the affluent seaside town, the centre caters for the rich and famous as well as successful business people.

"We jealously guard the privacy of our clients," says Dr David Sack, the centre's chief operating officer.

"We want to ensure that they have the time and the opportunity to get better from their addictions without intrusions so we work very hard to make sure that we don't have our clients on TV or used in the media in any way."

Very relaxed

The centre's focus on privacy meant BBC News was unable to interview any of its current clients, although we spotted a major TV star in the dining room.

In the past, the secluded setting has proved enticing for the tabloid media.

"We have paparazzi who will walk two miles in on public land so that they can try to get a photograph over the mountains behind our buildings," says Dr Sack.

"But you know most people try to respect other people's treatment."

It is an extremely relaxed setting, akin to a residential home for the elderly. There are no locks on the doors and the clients are free to leave at any time.

The atmosphere is homely with a comfortable living room area and a large family kitchen.

Celebrity clients are treated in exactly the same way as everyone else. They take part in group therapy sessions and help with the chores such as cooking and laundry.

But the underlying problems that result in Hollywood's elite seeking help, may be different.

"We think that success creates new pressures and demands on people that add to their anxiety and make them more susceptible to alcohol and other drugs," says Dr Sack.

"We think that being a celebrity, where your privacy is invaded, where you don't have the quiet time and downtime that everybody needs, adds to that problem.

"We also think that highly creative people are at greater risk for psychiatric disorders including depression, bipolar disorder and substance abuse and alcohol."

Elizabeth Clopton worked behind the scenes in Hollywood when she sought help at Promises for a drug and alcohol problem.

Five years on she has beaten her addiction and has taken up an administrative job at the rehabilitation centre.

Like 90% of the clients, Ms Clopton was not a celebrity.

"There were people that I was here with who were in the news and it didn't matter because when you're in your group and you're all talking together, you're all equal and you're all fighting the same disease," she says.

"We all come in with our issues and some of them might have been in the tabloids—and the rest of us—we might not have had news stories written about us, but our issues might be just as big."

"If someone has someone blogging about them or reporting on them it doesn't mean that their issues are necessarily any worse, it doesn't mean that their disease is any worse it just means that they're in the public eye."

Equine therapy

A standard programme of rehabilitation at Promises lasts for 31 days. The cost starts at approximately $ 54,000 (£ 35,000) and rises to about $ 90,000 (£ 59,000) depending on whether the client wants a private bedroom. Many opt to share two-bed suites.

The property enjoys stunning views of the Pacific ocean, with outdoor areas for sitting, meditation and yoga.

The centre uses western medicine and psychotherapy as well as alternative approaches to help people with their addictions.

Equine therapy involves introducing the client to horses, at a local stable, for grooming and petting.

"A lot of it is about self-esteem and self-loathing," says Gary Troxell, who is an equine assistance psychotherapist.

"Coming out here and connecting with something living is huge, because it's a beginning for a lot of folks. They get to connect with a 1200 lb animal. That's power... a good spiritual power too."

Over the years there have been high profile cases of celebrities falling off the wagon or failing to complete the programme.

Centres such as Promises have found themselves the butt of comedians' jokes ao Hollywood actors and musicians follow what almost seems like a rite of passage into rehab.

It is a problem Dr Sack knows will not go away in the near future.

"The proportion of people with drug and alcohol problems is not decreasing-if anything, it's increasing," he says.

"I think what we want to do is to make sure that the people we help get better and stay better. And that's really our goal. [1]

http://news.bbc.co.uk/2/hi/entertainment/8653568.stm

Vocabulary

Match each word to its definition.

1. rehabilitation ( )   a. highly attractive and able to arouse hope or desire

2. affluent ( )   b. a freelance photographer who aggressively pursues celebrities for the purpose of taking candid photographs

3. seclude ( )   c. (medicine) the act of caring for someone (as by medication or remedial training etc.)

4. enticing ( )   d. the restoration of someone to a useful place in society

5. paparazzi ( )   e. keep away from others

6. therapy ( )   f. having an abundant supply of money or possessions of value

7. elite ( )   g. easily impressed emotionally

8. susceptible ( )   h. continuous and profound contemplation or musing on a subject or series of subjects of a deep or abstruse nature

9. meditation ( )   i. any of various kinds of wheeled vehicles drawn by a horse or tractor

10. wagon ( )   j. a group or class of persons enjoying superior intellectual or social or economic status

Discussion

Discuss the following questions with your class.

1. Are you interested in celebrity's news?

2. In your opinion, how to protect celebrities' privacy?

3. How do you keep mental healthy?

4. Which one is more important, mental health or physical health?

Section C

Growing Conversion of Movies to 3-D Draws Mixed Reactions

By Brooks Barnes

April 2, 2010

LOS ANGELES—For weeks, Hollywood has sat in judgment of a last-second decision by Warner Brothers to convert its two-dimensional "Clash of the Titans" into 3-D after filming was finished. James Cameron cried sacrilege, Michael Bay said such quickie conversions resulted in "fake 3-D" and fanboy bloggers lambasted Warner and urged people to skip it.

But what about regular moviegoers—would they even notice anything amiss with the movie's 3-D?

It's no small question for Hollywood. With at least 70 movies in the 3-D pipeline—including many similar conversion projects—studios and theater owners are betting heavily that audiences will snap up increasingly expensive 3-D tickets. Mr. Cameron, whose "Avatar" sparked this fervor by racking up nearly $ 2.7 billion in global ticket sales, fretted to Deadline.com that Warner is "expecting the same result, when in fact they will probably work against the adoption of 3-D, because they'll be putting out an inferior product."

"Clash of the Titans," a $ 122 million remake of the campy 1981 original, opened in wide release on Friday, and early feedback indicates that Joe and Jane

Moviegoer don't really see what all the fuss is about. Indeed, despite the negative media coverage of the film, box office forecasters say the picture is on track to sell between $ 60 million and $ 70 million in tickets by Monday—a very robust result.

"I thought the 3-D quality was really good," said Eric Shimp as he left a showing of "Clash of the Titans" at the AMC Century City 15 in Los Angeles. Mr. Shimp, who works in the automotive industry, added, "The ticket prices are ridiculous, but it does leave you feeling like you've just seen a spectacle."

Sharle Kochman, a cosmetologist, said as she left the theater that she thought the 3-D quality was on a par with "Avatar," and Lauren Shotwell, a music executive, said she noticed none of the tell-tale signs of a 3-D conversion: blurriness, double images (called "ghosting"), flat backgrounds. "During the computer-generated parts the 3-D looked totally fine," Ms. Shotwell said.

Twitter feedback was more mixed, with seemingly regular folks squaring off against the geekier variety. " 'Clash of the Titans' in 3D was a great movie had fun," wrote TaliaMenacho. Radharc countered: "Now that 'Clash of the Titans' is actually out I can finally say that whatever you do, see it in 2D. The post conversion to 3D isn't too hot."

Many directors are wary.

"The tidal wave of rush-job post-conversions to 3-D worries me, as it does a lot of filmmakers, because the results are often sketchy and nowhere near as immersive as in-camera 3-D photography," said Shawn Levy, the director of "Night at the Museum" and the coming comedy "Date Night," starring Tina Fey and Steve Carell. "Filmmakers have to resist the current frenzy for all things 3-D in order to first assess whether the movie's tone and subject matter organically benefit from it."

It remains too early to tell whether audiences will rebel at 3-D ("Avatar") and what some experts are calling 3-D Lite (movies shot the normal way and converted afterward). More tea leaves will be available next weekend. If interest in the 3-D version of "Clash of the Titans" drops sharply, analysts will view that as a signal of negative word of mouth. It's entirely possible, of course, that audiences will complain about the 3-D when they really just didn't like the story.

Another movie shot in 2-D and converted later—Walt Disney's "Alice in Wonderland"—certainly did not suffer at the box office, selling about $ 663 million in tickets worldwide.

The worry, as Mr. Cameron noted, is that studios will quickly train consumers to be more selective when it comes to 3-D, especially as ticket prices rise. Last week, several large movie theater chains lifted 3-D ticket prices 15 to 25 percent. As a result, many moviegoers in cities like New York and Los Angeles will now pay $ 19.50 each to see certain 3-D screenings. Typically, theaters charge an extra $ 3 to $ 5 for tickets to 3-D movies.

Studios, eager to chase 3-D revenue as DVD sales continue to decline, are scrambling to release as many movies in the format as they can, lest the current appetite for 3-D proves as ephemeral as the last one. The film business became fascinated with 3-D in the 1950s, only to watch its popularity die as audiences balked at the bulky glasses and jerky, stomach-churning camera movements.

The latest 3-D technology is supposed to be new and improved; at least that is how Hollywood has sold it to audiences. Digital projectors deliver precision images, eliminating headaches and nausea, while plastic glasses have replaced the cardboard. Most important, say filmmakers, new equipment allows movies to be built in 3-D from the ground up, providing a more immersive and realistic viewing experience, not one based just on occasional visual gimmicks.

But nearly every studio is now considering shortcuts. At 20th Century Fox a 3-D conversion of the coming "Chronicles of Narnia: Voyage of the Dawn Treader" is being weighed. Warner Brothers will convert both halves of its upcoming "Harry Potter and the Deathly Hallows." Mr. Bay has said that Paramount is pressuring him to give his third "Transformers" installment the treatment.

Conversion costs anywhere from $ 5 million to $ 30 million a movie, depending on the complexity.

Technology companies say the conversion process is being unfairly judged.

"I kind of rolled my eyes at first, but once I saw the tests I was really startled at how good this can look," said Rob Hummel, chief executive of Prime Focus North America, which retrofitted "Clash of the Titans."

"We're not the only ones who think that," he added. "Our phone is ringing off the hook with 911 calls from studios to do conversions."

Prime Focus introduced its conversion technology in July. Although the process is complex and largely proprietary, it involves computer software that determines which objects are in front of others—Actor A is walking in front of Actor B. The image in front is then digitally brought even farther forward.

Jim Dorey, editor of Marketsaw.com, a blog devoted to the medium, ultimately thinks the quickie "Clash" conversion was a mistake. But unlike many technophiles he is not closing the door on the retrofitting process.

"If the right money is spent and you take your time, then native 3-D and converted 3-D can both be exceptional," Mr. Dorey said. "Even when it's not very well done I suspect most consumers will find it passable."

http://www.nytimes.com/2010/04/03/movies/03threed.html

Discussion

Discuss the following questions with your class.

1. What do you know about 3-D movie?

2. Do you think it is necessary to convert two-dimensional movies into 3-D?

3. In you opinion, what factors contribute to a successful movie, director, actor/ actress, or technology?

4. Comparing with staying at home to watch a movie on the internet, what are the advantages of going to the cinema to watch a film?

Unit Three

Environment

Section A

Gulf Oil Spill Could Be Unprecedented Disaster—Obama

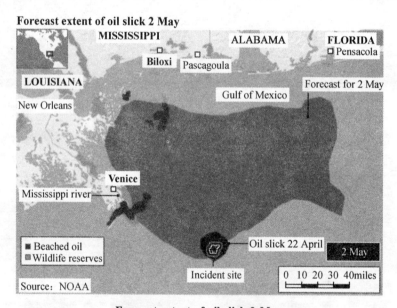

Forecast extent of oil slick 2 May

The Issue in the News

President Obama's exhortation to the American people is a simple one: Trust government. Yet faced with his first major disaster—the BP oil spill—Obama is facing a critical test of his philosophy: If the federal government can do so much, why can't it stop the slow-motion Deepwater Horizon disaster in the Gulf? The White House says the response to the spill disaster has been unprecedented with Obama in charge from the beginning, corralling resources and holding BP, which leased the Deepwater Horizon rig, accountable. What's more, the Oil Pollution Act of 1990 mandates the current command structure that puts BP at the top of the relief effort.

Points to Notice

As you read, pay attention to the following facets and information mentioned in this piece of news:

● Obama would do whatever it takes to clean up the oil

● Louisiana Governor has warned that the spill threatens the way of life in the state

● BP has said it will honor legitimate claims for damages

Text

3 May 2010

US President Barack Obama has described a sprawling oil slick in the Gulf of Mexico[1] as a "potentially unprecedented" environmental disaster.

Speaking in Louisiana, Mr Obama said his government would do whatever it takes to clean up the oil, adding that BP[2] was responsible and must pay.

He said the focus was now on preventing any further damage to the Gulf coast.

BP says it will be at least a week before temporary measures to stem the leak are in place.

But it could take up to three months to drill relief wells that could fully contain the spillage, Interior Secretary Ken Salazar warned on Sunday.

The BP-operated Deepwater Horizon rig sank on 22 April, two days after a huge explosion that killed 11 workers.

Louisiana Governor Bobby Jindal has warned the spill threatens the way of life in his state.

Mr Obama flew to Louisiana on Sunday to see for himself the damage.

Speaking in the town of Venice, he said: "We're dealing with a massive and potentially unprecedented environmental disaster.

"The oil that is still leaking from the well could seriously damage the economy and the environment of our Gulf states.

"And it could extend for a long time. It could jeopardise the livelihoods of thousands of Americans who call this place home."

'Mitigate the damage'

The president said the slick was now nine miles (14km) off the coast of south-eastern Louisiana.

And he warned: "BP is responsible for this leak. BP will be paying the bill."

BP chief executive Tony Hayward, who is in Louisiana to oversee the company's clean-up, said: "I agree with the president that the top priority right now is to stop the leak and mitigate the damage."

The company has said it will honour legitimate claims for damages.

BP chairman Lamar McKay said they hoped to lower a hastily made dome a mile below the surface to cap the wellhead in the next six to eight days, as a short-term option.

There have been warnings that within weeks the spill, if unchecked, could eclipse the 1989 Exxon Valdez disaster as the worst in US history.

The Louisiana wetlands host a multi-billion-dollar fishing industry and are a prime spawning area for fish, shrimp, crabs and oysters.

Mississippi, Alabama and Florida have also declared a state of emergency and are considering their legal options.

http://news. bbc. co. uk/2/hi/8657100. stm

Online Resources

http://news. bbc. co. uk/weather/hi/climate/newsid _ 8657000/8657167. stm

http://news. bbc. co. uk/2/hi/americas/8657556. stm

http://news. bbc. co. uk/2/hi/in _ pictures/8657315. stm

Vocabulary

1.	unprecedented	*adj.*	前所未有的;空前的;没有先例的
2.	sprawling	*adj.*	蔓延的,不规则地伸展的
3.	spillage	*n.*	the act of allowing a fluid to escape 漏,溢出,溢出液
4.	stem	*vi.*	stop the flow of a liquid 堵住,阻止;逆……而行
5.	jeopardize	*vt.*	pose a threat to; present a danger to 危害,使受危困,使陷危地
6.	mitigate	*vt.*	lessen or to try to lessen the seriousness or extent of 镇静,缓和,减轻
7.	legitimate	*adj.*	authorized, sanctioned by, or in accordance with law 合法的,正当的,合理的,世袭的
8.	hastily	*adv.*	in a hurried or hasty manner 匆忙地,急速地
9.	eclipse	*vt.*	exceed in importance; outweigh 形成日或月食,使……黯然失色
10.	shrimp	*n.*	disparaging terms for small people 虾,瘦小的人事物
11.	crab	*n.*	decapod having eyes on short stalks and a broad flattened carapace with a small abdomen folded under the thorax and pincers 蟹
12.	oyster	*n.*	marine mollusks having a rough irregular shell; found on the sea bed mostly in coastal waters 牡蛎

Language Notes

1. **The Gulf of Mexico**: the ninth largest body of water in the world. It is a partially landlocked ocean basin largely surrounded by the North American continent and the island of Cuba.

2. **BP**: British-based global energy company which is the third largest energy company and the fourth largest company in the world. The name "BP" is the initials of one of the company's former legal names, British Petroleum.

Exercises

✉ Vocabulary and Expressions

A. Idioms and Expressions

Fill in the blanks with the correct idiom or expression.

1. in place：in the original or natural place or site 在适当的位置,正确的,恰当的

I don't think his advice in place.

2. for oneself：独自一人;为自己

He can't do such a thing for himself.

He soon won a reputation for himself.

1. He is above taking profits _____.

2. I like to have everything _____.

3. In business, it's every man _____.

B. Vocabulary

Fill in the blanks with the words given below. Change the form where necessary.

| unprecedented stemmed jeopardize hastily |
| mitigate legitimate sprawling eclipsed |

1. I really fail to understand what actuated you to give up such a promising post so _____.

2. If you are rude to the boss, it may _____ your chance of success.

3. Our happiness was soon _____ by the terrible news.

4. The air crash caused an _____ number of deaths.

5. The government is trying to _____ the effects of inflation.

6. I'm not sure that his business is strictly _____.

7. His fist sent the robber _____ on the ground.

8. Our ship _____ on against the current.

Exploring Content

A. Match the person with his own statement.

Tony Hayward   Barack Obama   Ken Salazar   Bobby Jindal   Lamar McKay

1. _____ They hoped to lower a hastily made dome a mile below the surface to cap the wellhead in the next six to eight days, as a short-term option.

2. _____ The focus was now on preventing any further damage to the Gulf coast.

3. _____ The slick was now nine miles (14km) off the coast of south-eastern Louisiana.

4. _____ The spill threatens the way of life in his state.

5. _____ I agree with the president that the top priority right now is to stop the leak and mitigate the damage.

6. _____ It could take up to three months to drill relief wells that could fully contain the spillage.

B. Find the synonym in the reading.

1. Find a word in Paragraph 1 that means *possibly.* _____

2. Find a word in Paragraph 4 that means *momentary.* _____

3. Find a word in Paragraph 7 that means *present a danger to.*

_____

4. Find a word in Paragraph 14 that means *a person responsible for the administration of a business.* _____

5. Find a word in Paragraph 14 that means *precedency.* _____

Translation

Translate the following sentences into Chinese.

1. Speaking in Louisiana, Mr. Obama said his government would do whatever it takes to clean up the oil, adding that BP was responsible and must pay.

2. He said the focus was now on preventing any further damage to the Gulf coast.

3. BP says it will be at least a week before temporary measures to stem the leak are in place.

4. Speaking in the town of Venice, he said: "We're dealing with a massive and potentially unprecedented environmental disaster."

5. Mississippi, Alabama and Florida have also declared a state of emergency and are considering their legal options.

 Cloze

Complete the following short passage by choosing proper words from the word bank provided.

migration	neither	shelf	wildlife	number	participated	either	jeopardy
shelter	warn	casualties	flock	anticipated	wildness	appoint	

Despite the images of oil-soaked pelicans flooding the media in recent weeks, wildlife experts say the toll on sea birds from BP's Gulf Coast oil spill is smaller than was __1__, so far. That is expected to change drastically for the worse. Scientists __2__ that as shifting weather and sea conditions conspire with the dynamics of avian life cycles, a tremendous __3__ of birds will soon be put in __4__. In the coming weeks, millions of waterfowl and other birds that __5__ to the Gulf Coast on their annual fall __6__ will arrive in the region __7__ to roost for the winter or to make brief stopovers en route farther south. With toxic crude still gushing from the floor of the Gulf of Mexico and streaks of the slick creeping inexorably farther inland, many more birds and other wildlife that nest, feed and find __8__ on shore are likely to become __9__. "To this point, we haven't seen a lot of oiled wildlife based on the size of the spill," U. S. Fish and Wildlife Service biologist Catherine Berg said. "(But) there's still a lot of oil out there. There's still a lot of __10__ in the area."

Discussion

Discuss the following questions with your class.

1. What kind of role does Obama government play in this issue?

2. What challenge does BP have to face?

3. What's the top priority in the gulf oil spill?

4. What does the spill issue threaten?

■ Section B ■

Copenhagen Climate Summit Wasn't a Flop, Reports Say

Largely criticized for failing to produce a treaty to curb warming, the meeting did generate significant emission-reducing commitments from countries, including China and India, several analysts say.

By Jim Tankersley

April 1, 2010

Washington—The Copenhagen climate summit, roundly dubbed a failure when it ended last year, may actually have sparked significant steps toward curbing global warming, according to some environmentalists and financial analysts.

Analyses from groups, including Deutsche Bank, the Natural Resources Defense Council and the liberal Center for American Progress, are challenging the snap indictment of the December conference, which drew wide criticism for failing to produce a new treaty to limit greenhouse gas emissions.

Now, after adding up the individual commitments from the countries at the summit and translating them into tons of greenhouse gas emissions that will be kept out of the atmosphere, several analysts say the Copenhagen conference appears to have generated even more pledged emissions reduction than the 1997 Kyoto Protocol, the first major international climate agreement.

The conference was "no failure" and produced "the highest number of new government initiatives ever recorded... in a four-month period," Deutsche Bank, which tracks climate policy as part of its research on clean energy investments, declared in a March report.

The bank attributed 154 new domestic policies to the talks, which were attended by representatives from 193 countries.

"Copenhagen served to raise awareness of the problem all over the world, and that in turn forced governments to focus on the issue," Kevin Parker, the bank's global head of asset management, wrote in the report.

Trevor Houser, a visiting fellow at the Peterson Institute for International Economics who worked on the State Department's negotiating team in Copenhagen, tallied the commitments from the accord and projected their effect through century's end.

Under what he called "reasonable" economic and technical assumptions of what each country could expect to keep doing, Houser concluded that the Copenhagen commitments would give the world a 50% chance of holding warming to 2 degrees Celsius by 2100, the level many scientists say is needed to avert catastrophic warming.

The Center for American Progress estimated the pledges would take the world two-thirds of the way to "climate safety."

But as is virtually everything related to climate change, the findings are hotly disputed.

"We haven't seen any action yet" as a result of the accord, said Bill McKibben, director of the climate action group 350. org and an early critic of the Copenhagen result. "Not only did they not agree on anything... the stuff they didn't agree upon was spectacularly insufficient."

The two-week conference, which included more than 100 heads of state, ended with only a skeletal deal, which spanned only a few pages.

It allowed countries to set voluntary and nonbinding pledges to reduce emissions by 2020. It set up international monitoring of those pledges, and it promised to send billions of dollars from wealthy nations to the developing world to help poorer nations reduce emissions and adapt to warming temperatures.

Critics said neither the cuts nor the money sufficed to avert the likelihood of catastrophic climate change.

"A successful outcome from Copenhagen would have required a minimum of two commitments from developed countries: deep cuts in greenhouse gas emissions and adequate funds to address climate change in developing countries," the environmental group Friends of the Earth wrote soon after the summit. "The Copenhagen Accord didn't deliver either."

President Obama conceded when he announced the accord that it did not go as far as scientists had urged.

But he contended the agreement was a crucial starting point, particularly because it was the first international deal to win commitments from China and India, whose booming economies will produce much of the world's emissions growth this century.

Administration officials have ramped up that argument in recent months, as more than 100 countries signed onto the accord, including 60 that pledged to reduce emissions.

"What we're starting to learn," said Joe Aldy, special assistant to the president for energy and environment, "is, with this approach where we say to countries, come forward and... make public your emissions targets and actions, it is creating almost a positive dynamic now, where countries look at their peers and say, 'Wait, I should do something. ' "

Several analysts say those pronouncements, while unenforceable internationally, have begun to spur domestic policies to reduce emissions in China, Brazil and other nations.

Houser said in an interview after the summit that "the focus has moved from a binding international agreement to meaningful domestic policy, which is what ultimately matters. International agreements don't in and of themselves produce emissions cuts. Domestic policies do. "

The biggest domestic question remains the United States, where emission limits are pending in the Senate. Sen. John F. Kerry (D-Mass.), one of the architects of the climate bill, said the accord had not soured any colleagues on the legislation, which he is pitching more as an economic and national security boost than an emission-reducer.

The Deutsch Bank analysis shows huge reductions pledged by China and Brazil but little from America.

"The U.S. contribution to planned emission reductions has been dismal," it said, adding: "While Congress stumbles, America continues to fall behind."

http://www. latimes. com/news/nationworld/nation/la-na-copenhagen 2-2010apr02,0,4785480. story

Vocabulary

Match each word to its definition.

1. flop　　　　　(　)　a. a useful or valuable quality
2. indictment　(　)　b. in a spectacular manner
3. asset　　　　(　)　c. a complete failure
4. avert　　　　(　)　d. behave violently, as if in state of a great anger
5. spectacularly (　)　e. an accusation of wrongdoing
6. concede　　　(　)　f. prevent from happening
7. ramp　　　　(　)　g. not capable of being brought about by compulsion
8. unenforceable (　)　h. acknowledge defeat

Discussion

Discuss the following questions with your class.

1. Do you think Copenhagen climate conference is a failure or not? And why?
2. What has been solved in this conference?
3. What does the outcome from Copenhagen require?
4. What does the Copenhagen Accord mean for the developing countries like China and India?

■ **Section C** ■

Can the Rainforests Be Saved without a Plan?

By Christoph Seidler

January 26, 2010

The West wants to direct billions toward protecting forest lands, but the lack of any standardized rules and enforcement methods could lead to disaster. Experts warn that the wrong people might benefit from the money and argue indigenous peoples, not bureaucrats, should watch over the rainforests.

It would seem like fairly simple logic: If you want to help protect the environment, help save the forests. Huge amounts of carbon dioxide are stored in plants and the soil beneath them. So, clearing forests using slash-and-burn techniques only succeeds in releasing harmful CO_2 and methane gas into the atmosphere.

Even if it is still difficult to precisely quantify the carbon footprint of deforestation, it would still only seem logical that there would be some sort of financial reward for protecting the forests. One mechanism, known as "Reducing Emissions from Deforestation and Forest Degradation," or REDD—envisions a system that would allow industrialized countries to pay developing and newly industrializing countries to preserve large tracts of forest land. But a newly published report suggests that the REDD program might also give rise to its own set of problems.

The report was put together by the Washington-based Rights and Resources Initiative (RRI), whose partners include the International Union for Conservation of Nature (IUCN) and the Center for International Forestry Research (CIFOR). "The states have pledged heaps of money without agreeing to any framework or standards for REDD," RRI coordinator Andy White told SPIEGEL ONLINE. As White sees it, the fact that the world failed to reach a climate agreement in Copenhagen has meant that there are no rules or enforcement measures in place for properly implementing projects aimed at protecting forests.

Indeed, scientists at RRI fear that governments of developing and newly industrializing countries might be tempted to disregard the rights of local communities in order to get their hands on the money of investors as quickly as possible.

Billions in Promises

The amount of money involved is enormous. So far, there have only been pilot projects, but some industrialized nations have announced plans to devote very large amounts of money to protecting forests. For example, in Copenhagen, six nations—the United States, Australia, Norway, Great Britain, France and Japan—pledged to make approximately $ 3.5 billion (£ 2.5 billion) available before 2012 for REDD-related projects. In the next few years, this figure could get even higher, particularly if more countries decide to join in the effort.

REDD is attractive to industrialized nations for a number of reasons. First, it helps them protect the environment more effectively. Second, it gives rich countries a chance to spare themselves from having to take unpopular domestic measures by investing in climate protection abroad. But a run on the forest-protection projects could destroy the CO_2 trading systems that are already operating in places like Europe. A flood of cheap emissions certificates from REDD projects could drive the price of emitting greenhouse gases way down.

White and his colleagues fear that, as long as there are no uniform rules for the projects, the downpour of REDD-related funding might have problematic consequences. For example, they warn that the measures might lead to more corruption and to indigenous populations being deprived of their rights. For example, in the worst-case scenario, they fear that REDD funds could end up in the coffers of lumber companies that have managed to get their hands on forest licenses beforehand in some sort of shady way.

Slim Chances for Universal Regulation

Rules related to protecting forests are theoretically supposed to come as part of a larger global pact on climate change. But ever since the chaos surrounding last December's climate change summit in Copenhagen, it's been anyone's guess whether such regulations will ever take shape. Given this state of affairs, France and Norway have announced that they will host meetings this year focused on hammering out framework conditions specifically for projects related to protecting forests. Although the meetings will not result in any system of universal regulation, they should succeed in getting key nations—such as Brazil and Indonesia—onboard. Still, White is convinced that only a coordinated approach for a REDD system will have any chance of bringing about positive results on the global level.

The main demand of the researchers at RRI are that, to the greatest extent possible, local communities be put in charge of looking after the forests rather than bureaucrats drawn from the administrative ranks. "The level of deforestation is the highest in government forests," Andy White says. On the other hand, he notes that the lowest wood-harvesting rates are found in areas administered by local inhabitants—and that these rates are even lower than those in national parks. Likewise, White points to "encouraging signs of progress" in land-reform efforts in China and Brazil that benefit local groups.

Some of these efforts have met with apparent success. For example, there have been significant reductions in deforestation rates in the Amazon rainforest. During the climate summit in Copenhagen, Almir Surui, the chief of the Surui tribe in the western Brazilian state of Rondonia, advocated for allowing his people to be put in charge of their own forest. And, as he put it, since his tribe watched over the rain forests, it should also get the money for doing so. His tribe has come up with a 50-year plan aimed at allowing them to keep living in a traditional way within an intact forest.

'A Major Opportunity'

Andy White is calling for the forest protection issues to be resolved by the end of the year. As he sees it, REDD continues to present "a major opportunity." Likewise, many developing and newly industrialized countries continue to be interested in the approach. If nothing else, they still see it as an indication of how willing wealthier nations are to invest in climate protection.

But, as one example in South America shows, it's clear that there is only so much time left for negotiating. And in Ecuador, the government had been planning to forego tapping the enormous Ishpingo-Tambococha-Tiputini oilfields as long as it was adequately compensated for not doing so. The asking price was $ 3.5 billion (£ 2.5 billion) —or half of the estimated market price of the oil that could presumably be extracted over a 10-year period.

But a few days ago, President Rafael Correa expressed his displeasure at the current state of negotiations. As he put it, his country did not intend to let foreign powers impose their will on it. "What they want," Correa said, " is for all of the little birdies in the entire Amazon region to live happy lives while the people there starve to death. " The state-owned oil company Petroecuador is now reportedly preparing a tender for drilling in the oil reserves. The Chinese oil company Sinopec and its Brazilian competitor, Petrobas, are planning bids, according to the *Frankfurter Allgemeine Zeitung*.

http://www.spiegel.de/international/world/0,1518,674169,00.html

Discussion

Discuss the following questions with your class.

1. What can we do to help protect environment?

2. Why are industrialized nations interested in REDD?

3. What can people do to prevent deforestation?

4. What causes President Rafael Correa's displeasure?

Unit Four

Sports

Section A

Africa: As World Cup Opens, UN Celebrates the Power of Sport for Peace and Development

The Issue in the News

The result of winning bid to host the World Cup, the biggest of all sporting events, is that pitch fever has reached fever pitch in South Africa. Many hands have come together to build magnificent stadiums around the country, and what Blatter and President Zuma assure the public is that part of those billions of dollars that went into organizing the World Cup will be spent on educational and health care infrastructure, not only in South Africa but around Africa as well. It is amazing that a simple game could have brought this country of seeming opposites, and differences, and multi-hued, multi-linguistic cultures together.

Points to Notice

As you read, pay attention to the following facets and information mentioned in this piece of news:

- the critical role that sport plays in some vital issues
- the power of the World Cup
- Millennium Development Goals

Text

11 June 2010

The World Cup soccer tournament kicked off today in South Africa with the United Nations highlighting the critical role that sport plays in promoting both peace and development and in spurring action on a range of vital issues.

The UN is harnessing the power of the World Cup, which is being held for the first time in Africa, to advance a host of objectives from ensuring quality education and a clean environment to reducing hunger and disease.

Secretary-General Ban Ki-moon, who attended the World Cup opening ceremony and game today in Johannesburg[1], has described the event as a major landmark for the people of Africa, and a triumph for humanity.

Mr. Ban and the UN family are using the World Cup to make a major push for the Millennium Development Goals (MDGs)[2]——the eight targets world leaders have pledged to achieve by 2015.

"As we cheer the teams on the football pitch, let us remember: achieving the MDGs is not a spectator sport. It takes every one of us on the field," he said in remarks to the Sports for Peace Gala in Johannesburg on Tuesday night.

"If we work together, we can score a victory over poverty. We can defeat ignorance, discrimination and want. We can ensure every man and woman, every girl and boy has an opportunity on the playing field of life," he stated.

Wilfried Lemke, the Secretary-General's Special Adviser on Sport for Development and Peace, stressed the opportunities presented by mega-events such as the World Cup and the Olympic Games to boost social, economic and environmental development.

"Sport has the unique power to attract, mobilize and inspire and is by far, the most popular activity in which youth engage," he said ahead of the month-long World Cup.

A host of UN agencies are undertaking efforts in connection with the event, including a major initiative to 'green' the World Cup and help reduce carbon emissions involving the UN Environment Programme (UNEP) and the South African Government.

The UN Children's Fund (UNICEF) has a series of partnerships and programmes to harness the power of sport to promote children's rights. It includes a programme to enable young people in Rwanda and Zambia who would otherwise not have the chance to watch the World Cup matches to do so via large open-air screens and projectors.

A massive "Red Card" campaign has also been launched to target child abuse, exploitation, child sex tourism and trafficking.

Other UN events and campaigns include those addressing racism and intolerance, child labour, violence and women and girls, and HIV/AIDS prevention, treatment, care and support.

http://allafrica. com/stories/201006111018. html

Online Resources

http://allafrica. com/view/group/main/main/id/00011508. html

Vocabulary

1. highlight   *vt.*   move into the foreground to make more visible or prominent

			加亮,强调,使……显得重要,照亮;
		n.	加亮区,精彩部分,最重要的细节或事件,闪光点
2.	harness	*vt.*	exploit the power of 束以马具,披上甲胄,利用(产生动力)
3.	objective	*n.*	the goal intended to be attained 目标,目的
4.	landmark	*n.*	the position of a prominent or well-known object in a particular landscape 陆标,地界标,里程碑,划时代的事
5.	humanity	*n.*	the quality of being humane 人类,人性,人道,慈爱
6.	mobilize	*vt.*	make ready for action or use 动员,赋予可动性,使流通
7.	emission	*n.*	the act of emitting; causing to flow forth 散发,发射,射出,发行
8.	initiative	*n.*	readiness to embark on bold new ventures 第一步,首创精神,主动权
9.	projector	*n.*	an optical instrument that projects an enlarged image onto a screen 放映机(探照灯)

Language Notes

1. **Johannesburg**: the largest city in South Africa. Johannesburg is the provincial capital of Gauteng, the wealthiest province in South Africa, having the largest economy of any metropolitan region in Sub-Saharan Africa. The city is one of the 40 largest metropolitan areas in the world, and is also the world's largest city not situated on a river, lake, or coastline.

2. **The Millennium Development Goals** (MDGs): eight international development goals that all 192 United Nations member states and at least 23 international organizations have agreed to achieve by the year 2015. They include reducing extreme poverty, reducing child mortality rates, fighting disease epidemics such as AIDS, and developing a global partnership for development.

Exercises

✉ Vocabulary and Expressions

A. Idioms and Expressions

Fill in the blanks with the correct idiom or expression.

1. kick off：commence officially 开球,开始

A sports personality was invited to kick off at the final.

2. spur on：give heart or courage to 鼓舞,鞭策

He was spurred on by ambition.

3. cheer on：show approval or good wishes by shouting 为……打气,激励……,向……喝彩

As the football match was in progress, we kept cheering on both teams.

4. by far：until now 到目前为止

The TV tower is by far the largest construction of our country.

1. He _____ at the thought of seeing her again.

2. She _____ her team to try harder.

3. I've seen some slow workers in my time but this lot are the slowest _____.

4. I'll ask Tessa to _____ the discussion.

B. Vocabulary

Fill in the blanks with the words given below. Change the form where necessary.

landmark objective projector emission humanity
initiative harness mobilize highlight

1. I put it all down to her hard work and _____.

2. Our ultimate _____ is the removal of all nuclear weapons.

3. Our country's in great danger; we must _____ the army.

4. China ought to make a greater contribution to _____ .

5. We can _____ the power of the wind to make electricity.

6. _____ of visible light by living organisms such as the firefly and various fish, fungi, and bacteria.

7. The film flew off the spool and wound itself round the _____ .

8. It is one of the _____ of the match.

9. Marble Arch is a famous London _____ .

Exploring Content

A. Fill in the blanks according to the passage.

1. Secretary-General Ban Ki-moon has described the opening of the World Cup as a _____ for the people of Africa, and a _____ for humanity.

2. "We can ensure every man and woman, every girl and boy has _____ ," Ban stated.

3. Wilfried Lemke stressed _____ presented by mega-events such as the World Cup and the Olympic Games to _____ .

4. The purpose of a series of partnerships and programmes taken by the UN Children's Fund is to _____ .

5. A massive "Red Card" campaign has been launched to target _____ , _____ , _____ and _____ .

B. Find the synonym in the reading.

1. Find a word in Paragraph 1 that means *vital*. _____

2. Find a word in Paragraph 1 that means *a sporting competition in which contestants play a series of games to decide the winner.* _____

3. Find a word in Paragraph 6 that means *unfair treatment of a person or group on the basis of prejudice.* _____

4. Find a word in Paragraph 7 that means *encourage*. _____

5. Find a word in Paragraph 11 that means *movement*. _____

✉ Translation

Translate the following sentences into Chinese.

1. The UN is harnessing the power of the World Cup, which is being held for the first time in Africa, to advance a host of objectives from ensuring quality education and a clean environment to reducing hunger and disease.

2. Secretary-General Ban Ki-moon, who attended the World Cup opening ceremony and game today in Johannesburg, has described the event as a major landmark for the people of Africa, and a triumph for humanity.

3. Mr. Ban and the UN family are using the World Cup to make a major push for the Millennium Development Goals (MDGs)—the eight targets world leaders have pledged to achieve by 2015.

4. As we cheer the teams on the football pitch, let us remember: achieving the MDGs is not a spectator sport.

5. Sport has the unique power to attract, mobilize and inspire and is by far, the most popular activity in which youth engage.

✉ Cloze

Complete the following short passage by choosing proper words from the word bank provided.

| crowns win elementary figure fundamental throughout shape effect |
| objective Brazilian prepare Brazil confident influential subjective |

Brazil's __1__ playmaker Kaka says his primary objective for the upcoming year is to help his country __2__ their sixth World Cup in South Africa. The Real Madrid star and fellow __3__ countrymen have been drawn into what many have described as the "Group of Death", alongside Portugal, Ivory Coast and North Korea, but he is __4__ the many time champions can lift another one of football's most prestigious __5__. "The World Cup is surely the principle __6__. The World Cup will be the continuation of all the hard work a player does at club level," he told Brazilian paper O Stadio. "I have to __7__ well with Real Madrid so that I can get to South Africa in good __8__." He added: "Many things can happen __9__ the tournament. You can win or lose, but if we go there having prepared well then we have a great chance," he added. "We have to use the two weeks of preparation well as this will be ___10___ for the squad to win the tournament."

Discussion

Discuss the following questions with your class.

1. What kind of role does sport play in promoting peace and development?

2. What can the UN family use the power of the World Cup to do?

3. Why does Secretary-General Ban Ki-moon describe the World Cup as a triumph for humanity?

4. What kind of power does sport have for you?

■ **Section B** ■

Triumph Overcomes Tragedy after Host Nation Takes Games to Its Heart

By Rick Broadbent

March 1, 2010

Vancouver 2010 will be remembered as a success

Few people remember Jorg Oberhammer these days. The physician for the Austria team was preparing for the start of the giant slalom when he collided with a recreational skier and was thrown under a snow-grooming machine. He was crushed to death beneath a chairlift carrying the watching Pirmin Zurbriggen and Martin Hangl.

The former went on to take the bronze medal, but the latter collapsed under the emotion of what he had witnessed and withdrew, thus summing up the dilemma of what to do when human tragedy treads on the toes of sporting drama.

That was 1988, the previous time that the Olympics visited Canada. Fast forward to today and one wonders whether, for all the grief in Georgia and compassion in Canada, any neutral will remember Nodar Kumaritashvili in a few years' time. The death of the luger hours before the opening of the Vancouver Games might have been expected to cast a depression over all that followed, but instead we have seen the truth of the oft-maligned Bill Shankly aphorism that sport really can seem important than life and death.

That was never more evident than in Canada's manic 3-2 overtime victory over the United States in the men's ice hockey final last night. The host nation were 24 seconds from victory against a team who had pulled their goaltender, when Zach Parise made it 2-2. Enter Sidney Crosby, the pin-up boy of Canadian ice hockey, who had struggled to live up to his pre-Games billing, to score a goal that sent Canada into delirium.

It has often felt that the Olympics have been playing second fiddle to an ice hockey competition here. This is Canada's sport. "Destiny on ice," as the placards put it.

The win means Canada have 14 gold medals, more than any nation has managed at a Winter Games. The Canadian public has not so much embraced the Olympic circus as ravaged it behind the podium, and yes, the inflated medal target notwithstanding, Canada has owned that bloody thing.

They did not manage this many golds in ten Games from 1960 and indeed, in 1988, they were as bad as Britain and had none.

Many would have traded all the others for a repeat of the 2002 hockey triumph over the same opposition. Canada were again the better team on this occasion but had lost to the guts and goaltending of the US in the preliminaries. The Americans were belligerent again but when Jonathan Toews and Corey Perry put Canada clear, it looked straightforward until Ryan Kesler's deflection crept in. Cue Bedlam.

Parise created parity, Crosby made history.

In the hysteria it felt like official confirmation that the Olympics have been a huge success. The problems, and they have existed, despite certain claims, were forgotten. All that was left was sport. In years to come people will remember Alex Bilodeau winning Canada's first Olympic gold at home rather than the ripping up of 28,000 tickets because of safety fears on Cypress Mountain. They will recall the bravery of Joannie Rochette's bronze medal days after her mother's death and not the Olympic flame being locked away behind gates. Most of all, they will talk about the hockey.

When the dust settles on both the ice hockey and Vancouver, many questions will remain unanswered about Kumaritashvili's accident.

However, ultimately, these have been great Games where sport has ridden roughshod over the problems. They started with a human tragedy and ended in sporting catharsis. There is talk of Kumaritashvili's family suing the IOC, but as the hockey fans poured on to the city streets last night, the truth was that not even death has been able to get in the way of Canada's glory.

http://www.timesonline.co.uk/tol/sport/olympics/article7044623.ece

Vocabulary

Match each word with its definition.

1. delirium ( ) a. characteristic of an enemy or one eager to fight

2. dilemma ( ) b. make a pillaging or destructive raid on (a place), as in wartimes

3. neutral ( ) c. a short pithy instructive saying

4. luger ( ) d. state of uncertainty or perplexity especially as requiring a choice between equally unfavorable options

5. aphorism ( ) e. purging of emotional tensions

6. manic ( ) f. despite anything to the contrary

7. fiddle ( ) g. one who does not side with any party in a war or dispute

8. ravage ( ) h. affected with or marked by frenzy or mania uncontrolled by reason

9. notwithstanding ( ) i. state of violent mental agitation

10. belligerent ( ) j. someone who races the luge

11. roughshod ( ) k. commit fraud and steal from one's employer

12. catharsis ( ) l. unjustly domineering

Discussion

Discuss the following questions with your class.

1. Do you like watching hockey? If you like, can you introduce this match for us?

2. How much do you know about Jorg Oberhammer after reading this passage?

3. Can you talk about your feelings about the saying "Destiny on ice"?

4. Do you know the story behind Joannie Rochette's bronze medal?

■ Section C ■

Former IOC President Juan Antonio Samaranch Dies at 89

THE ASSOCIATED PRESS

April 21, 2010

BARCELONA—Juan Antonio Samaranch, a reserved but shrewd dealmaker whose 21-year term as president of the International Olympic Committee was marked by both the unprecedented growth of the games and its biggest ethics scandal, died Wednesday at a hospital. He was 89.

Samaranch, a courtly former diplomat who served as Spanish ambassador in Moscow, led the IOC from 1980 to 2001. He was considered one of the defining presidents for building the IOC into a powerful global organization and firmly establishing the Olympics as a world force.

Samaranch was admitted to the Quiron Hospital in Barcelona on Sunday after experiencing heart trouble and died early Wednesday.

"I cannot find the words to express the distress of the Olympic family," IOC president Jacques Rogge said. "I am personally deeply saddened by the death of the man who built up the Olympic Games of the modern era, a man who inspired me, and whose knowledge of sport was truly exceptional."

Rogge will be among a number of international figures to attend a special ceremony on Thursday morning before the funeral at Barcelona's cathedral later in the day.

Small in stature and shy by nature, Samaranch appeared uncomfortable appearing or speaking in public. But behind the scenes, he was a skilled and sometimes ruthless operator who could forge consensus in the often fractious Olympic movement and push IOC members to deliver exactly what he wanted.

Samaranch was also a lighting rod for critics, who attacked him for his ties to the Franco era in Spain, his autocratic style and the IOC's involvement in the Salt Lake City corruption scandal.

The Samaranch era was perhaps the most eventful in IOC history, spanning political boycotts, the end of amateurism and the advent of professionalism, the explosion of commercialization, a boom in growth and popularity of the games, the scourge of doping, and the Salt Lake crisis.

Samaranch had been bothered by health problems ever since stepping down nine years ago. He was hospitalized for 11 days in Switzerland with "extreme fatigue" in 2001 after returning from the IOC session in Moscow, where Belgium's Jacques Rogge was elected as his successor.

Samaranch was hospitalized shortly afterward in Barcelona for what was described as high blood pressure. He received regular dialysis treatment for kidney trouble.

He spent two days in a hospital in Madrid in 2007 after a dizzy spell, and underwent hospital checks in Monaco in October 2009 after feeling ill at a sports conference.

Despite the advancing age and medical troubles, Samaranch continued to travel to IOC meetings around the world. He looked increasingly frail in recent months.

Attending the IOC session at the Winter Games in Vancouver in February, he walked with the aid of a female assistant.

Even in retirement, Samaranch remained active in Olympic circles and tried to help Madrid secure the games of 2012 and 2016. Madrid finished third behind winner London and Paris in the 2005 vote for the 2012 Olympics, and second to

Rio de Janeiro for 2016.

Samaranch spoke during Madrid's presentation in Copenhagen on Oct. 2, 2009, virtually asking IOC members to send the games to the Spanish capital as a parting gift for an old man close to his final days.

"Dear colleagues, I know that I am very near the end of my time," Samaranch said. "I am, as you know, 89 years old. May I ask you to consider granting my country the honor and also the duty to organize the games and Paralympics in 2016."

In Moscow in 1980, as a little-known Spanish diplomat, Samaranch was elected the seventh president of the IOC, taking the most powerful job in global sports.

Twenty-one years later, as a well-known world figure, Samaranch returned to Moscow to finish his term-basking in the unprecedented popularity and riches of the games but still bearing the scars of the scandal that led to the ouster of 10 IOC members for receiving improper benefits from the 2002 Salt Lake bid committee.

While his closest friends said Samaranch was extremely emotional and sentimental, outwardly he remained cool and philosophical in his final days in office.

"I'm feeling OK," he said. "Life is life. There is a beginning and an end. This is the end of my presidency. I've known for a long time that this day was coming."

Even at the end of his Olympic reign in 2001, Samaranch worked hard to achieve three electoral victories as part of his final legacy: the awarding of the 2008 Olympics to Beijing, the election of Rogge as the new president, and the appointment of his son, Juan Antonio Jr., as an IOC member.

Samaranch retired as the second-longest serving president in the history of the IOC. Only Pierre de Coubertin, the French baron who founded the modern Olympics, was in office longer, serving for 29 years (1896-1925). American Avery Brundage served for 20 years (1952-72).

Samaranch was the last IOC leader to stay in office for so long. Under new rules, the maximum term for the president is 12 years (one eight-year mandate, plus the possibility of an additional four-year term). Rogge was re-elected unopposed to a second term in Copenhagen on Oct. 9, 2009, extending his period in office until 2013.

"After de Coubertin, there is no question that Samaranch stands head and shoulders above the other presidents in terms of his impact, not only on the Olympic Games but the place of the Olympic movement in the world," Olympic historian John MacAloon said.

Longtime Canadian IOC member Dick Pound, who finished third in the voting to Rogge, said Samaranch was one of three "great or defining presidents."

"De Coubertin to get it going, Brundage to hold it together through a very difficult period, and Samaranch to bring it from the kitchen table to the world stage," Pound said.

Samaranch spoke of the dramatic changes himself.

"You have to compare what is the Olympics today with what was the Olympics 20 years ago-that is my legacy," he said before his retirement. "It is much more important. Also, all our sources of finances are coming from private sources, not a single dollar from the government. That means we can assure our independence and autonomy."

"And the most important thing-it is easy to say but not to get-is the unity with the national Olympic committees and mainly with the international federations."

When Samaranch came to power in 1980, the IOC was virtually bankrupt and the Olympics were battered by boycotts, terrorism and financial troubles.

When he left, the IOC's coffers were bulging from billions of dollars in commercial revenues, the boycott era was over, and the games were firmly established as the world's favorite sports festival.

"He took a very badly fragmented, disorganized and impecunious organization and built it into a universal, united and financially and politically independent organization that has credibility, not only in the world of sport, but also in political circles," Pound said. "That's an enormous achievement to accomplish in 20 years."

Samaranch's presidency was also clouded by controversy. He was hounded by critics who said the games were over-commercialized and riddled with performance-enhancing drugs, and that he perpetuated the IOC image of a private club for a pampered elite.

British author Andrew Jennings, one of Samaranch's most virulent critics, wrote that "corruption became the lubrication of his Olympic industry" and that he "fleeced sport of its moral and monetary value."

Samaranch's reputation was scarred most of all by the Salt Lake City scandal, which led to the expulsion of six IOC members and resignation of four others who benefited from more than $ 1 million in cash, gifts, scholarships and other favors doled out during the Utah capital's winning bid for the 2002 Winter Games.

"What I regret, really regret, is what happened in Salt Lake City," he said.

"It obviously was a terrible blow to the organization, a terrible blow to him," MacAloon said. "He helped select many of the members who were found guilty of bribe-taking... It will be a lasting footnote to his presidency."

Samaranch used the crisis to push through a package of reforms designed to make the IOC more modern, open and democratic, including a ban on member visits to bid cities.

"We used this crisis to change the structure of the IOC," he said. "Maybe without this crisis, this would not have been possible."

In December 1999, Samaranch became the first IOC president to testify in Congress, enduring three hours of grilling on Capitol Hill from lawmakers skeptical of the reforms.

The 2000 Sydney Olympics, described by Samaranch as the best ever, seemed to take the heat off the IOC and restore faith in the games.

"We showed the world that the Olympic movement after the crisis is even stronger and with even more prestige than before," he said.

Pound said the scandal should not tarnish Samaranch's legacy.

"Once the corner is turned, the progress and the accomplishments in historical terms will supplant the fact that he was on watch when the Salt Lake problem arose," he said.

Samaranch's past was also a target for critics. Jennings and others denounced him for serving the Franco dictatorship in the 1960s and 1970s.

Samaranch angrily defended himself, saying it was up to Spaniards, not foreign journalists, to judge his record. He said he had only a modest role as director general of sports and parliamentary leader of the Falangist movement.

"Maybe some critics pushed me to be president for 21 years," Samaranch said. "I have to thank the critics. Maybe without the critics, I had to leave the IOC before."

Looking back, Samaranch acknowledged he could have retired earlier.

He considered stepping down after the 1992 Olympics in his home city of Barcelona and again after the centennial games in Atlanta in 1996. Each time, encouraged by his supporters, he chose to continue. Twice, he had the age limit changed to allow him to stay on.

As honorary IOC president for life, Samaranch remained active in the Olympic movement even after he stepped down. He chaired the board of the Olympic Museum in Lausanne and regularly attended IOC meetings around the world.

His wife, Maria Teresa, died from cancer in 2000 at 67, shortly after Samaranch presided over the opening ceremony of the Sydney Olympics. Samaranch flew to Barcelona to be at her bedside, but she died while he was still in the air. He later returned to Sydney for the remainder of the games.

In addition to his 50-year-old son, Samaranch is survived by a daughter, Maria Teresa. Both of his children along with his partner Luisa Sallent were by his side when he passed.

As a youth, Samaranch competed in field hockey, boxing and soccer. He became an IOC member in 1966 and was vice president from 1974—78.

Samaranch served as honorary chairman of La Caixa savings bank in Spain.

http://www.postcrescent.com/article/20100421/APC0101/100421022/1979/APCbusiness

Discussion

Discuss the following questions with your class.

1. How much do you know about Juan Antonio Samaranch?

2. What is Samaranch's contribution to the International Olympic Games?

3. What's the attitude of critics towards Samaranch?

4. What's your impression on Juan Antonio Samaranch after reading this passage?

Unit Five

Health

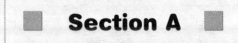

Green Spaces "Improve Health"

The best health benefits come from living less than a kilometre (0.62miles) from a green space.

The Issue in the News

Parks provide a much needed space for people to take part in organised or informal sports and provide recreational opportunities for those unable or unwilling to join a gym or leisure centre. We all know that a walk in the park can help clear the mind and the mental health benefits of parks and green space are well documented

Potential psychological and mental health benefits from exposure to nature are not limited to exposure in the countryside only; within urban and semi-urban settings, access to green, open spaces can have a beneficial effect.

There is increasing evidence that access to high quality green spaces can produce measurable improvements to stress levels in a relatively short space of time.

For every 10% increase in green space there was a reduction in health complaints equivalent to a reduction of 5 years age.

Points to Notice

As you read, pay attention to the following facets and information mentioned in this piece of news:

- Green spaces
- Health impact
- Anxiety disorders
- "Oasis" effect

Text

15 October 2009

There is more evidence that living near a "green space" has health benefits.

Research in the Journal of Epidemiology and Community Health says the impact is particularly noticeable in reducing rates of mental ill health.

The annual rates of 15 out of 24 major physical diseases were also significantly lower among those living closer to green spaces.

One environmental expert said the study confirmed that green spaces create "oases" of improved health around them.

The researchers from the VU University[1] Medical Centre in Amsterdam[2] looked at the health records of 350,000 people registered with 195 family doctors across the Netherlands[3].

Only people who had been registered with their GP for longer than 12 months were included because the study assumed this was the minimum amount of time people would have to live in an environment before any effect of it would be noticeable.

Health impact

The percentages of green space within a one and three kilometre (0. 62 and 1. 86 miles) radius of their home were calculated using their postcode.

On average, green space accounted for 42% of the residential area within one kilometre (0. 62 miles) radius and almost 61% within a three kilometre (1. 86 miles) radius of people's homes.

And the annual rates for 24 diseases in 7 different categories were calculated.

The health benefits for most of the diseases were only seen when the greenery was within a one kilometre (0. 62 miles) radius of the home.

The exceptions to this were anxiety disorders, infectious diseases of the digestive system and medically unexplained physical symptoms which were seen to benefit even when the green spaces were within three kilometres of the home.

The biggest impact was on anxiety disorders and depression.

Anxiety disorders

The annual prevalence of anxiety disorders for those living in a residential area containing 10% of green space within a one kilometre (0. 62 miles) radius of their home was 26 per 1000 whereas for those living in an area containing 90% of green space it was 18 per 1000.

For depression the rates were 32 per 1000 for the people in the more built up areas and 24 per 1000 for those in the greener areas.

The researchers also showed that this relation was strongest for children younger than 12.

They were 21% less likely to suffer from depression in the greener areas.

Two unexpected findings were that the greener spaces did not show benefits for high blood pressure and that the relation appeared stronger for people aged 46 to 65 than for the elderly.

The researchers think the green spaces help recovery from stress and offer greater opportunities for social contacts.

They say the free physical exercise and better air quality could also contribute.

Dr Jolanda Maas of the VU University Medical Centre in Amsterdam, said: "It clearly shows that green spaces are not just a luxury but they relate directly to diseases and the way people feel in their living environments."

"Most of the diseases which are related to green spaces are diseases which are highly prevalent and costly to treat so policy makers need to realise that this is something they may be able to diminish with green spaces."

Professor Barbara Maher of the Lancaster Environment Centre said the study confirmed that green spaces create oases of improved health around them especially for children.

She said: "At least part of this 'oasis' effect probably reflects changes in air quality.

"Anything that reduces our exposure to the modern-day 'cocktail' of atmospheric pollutants has got to be a good thing."

http://news. bbc. co. uk/2/hi/health/8307024. stm

Online Resources

http://www. greenspaceshome. com/

http://www. worldchanging. com/archives/009016. html

http://www. nursingtimes. net/whats-new-in-nursing/acute-care/green-spaces-to-improve-nurses-health-and-wellbeing/5009018. article

http://www. naturalengland. org. uk/ourwork/enjoying/health/default. aspx

Vocabulary

1. epidemiology *n.* the branch of medical science dealing with the transmission and control of disease 传染病学,流行病学

2. oasis *n.* a fertile tract in a desert (where the water table approaches the surface) 绿洲

3. confirm   *vt.*   establish or strengthen as with new evidence or facts 确定, 批准, 证实

4. radius   *n.*   半径, 半径范围

5. category   *n.*   a collection of things sharing a common attribute; classification 种类, 类别

6. disorder   *n.*   condition in which there is a disturbance of normal functioning 杂乱, 混乱

7. infectious   *adj.*   caused by infection or capable of causing infection; easily spread 传染的

8. digestive   *adj.*   relating to or having the power to cause or promote digestion 消化的

9. symptom   *n.*   subjective evidence of disease or physical disturbance 症状, 征兆

10. residential   *adj.*   used or designed for residence or limited to residences 住宅的, 与居住有关的

11. pollutant   *n.*   waste matter that contaminates the water or air or soil 污染物质

12. diminish   *vi.*   decrease in size, extent, or range 变少, 逐渐变细

13. prevalent   *adj.*   common at a particular time, in a particular place, or among a particular group of people 流行的, 普遍的

Language Notes

1. **the VU University**: The VU University Amsterdam has about 20,000 students, most of whom are full-time students. The university is located on a compact urban campus in the southern part of Amsterdam in the Buitenveldert district. Though a faith-based, private institution, the VU receives government funding on a parity basis with the public universities.

2. **Amsterdam**: the capital and largest city of the Netherlands, located in the province of North Holland in the west of the country. The city is the financial

and cultural capital of the Netherlands.

3. **Netherlands**: a constituent country of the Kingdom of the Netherlands, located in North-West Europe. It is a parliamentary democratic constitutional monarchy. The Netherlands borders the North Sea to the north and west, Belgium to the south, and Germany to the east.

Exercises

 Vocabulary and Expressions

A. Idioms and Expressions

Fill in the blanks with the correct idiom or expression.

1. on (the) average: generally; usually 总体来说

Health conditions were on the average pretty good.

2. relate something to something: to associate something to something 与……有关系

I relate this particular problem to the failure of the company to provide proper training.

3. suffer from something: to endure or experience unpleasantness, a disease, or a health condition 遭受

Jeff is suffering from the flu.

1. This point _____ what I just told you.

2. I'm afraid that you must _____ the disease until it has run its course.

3. Women _____ tend to be more interested in shopping than men.

B. Vocabulary

Fill in the blanks with the words given below. Change the form where necessary.

confirm	radius	postcode	category	infectious	digestive
symptom	disorder	residential	pollutant	diminish	prevalent

1. Although he is thin, he has good _____ power.

2. Seats are available in eight of the 10 price _____.

3. Common _____ of diabetes are weight loss and fatigue.

4. He looked around to _____ that he was alone.

5. Gradually the surrounding farmland turned _____.

6. Eye diseases are _____ in some tropical countries.

7. Flu is an _____ disease characterized by fever, aches and pains and exhaustion.

8. His illness _____ his health.

9. Discharge pipe take _____ away from the coastal area into the sea.

10. Wine cups and dishes lay about in _____ in the room.

✉ Exploring Content

A. Read the following statement. Then find five sentences in the reading text as the most convincing evidence to support it. Write them above the line.

Statement: Green spaces "improve health".

1. _____

2. _____

3. _____

4. _____

5. _____

B. Find the synonym in the reading.

1. Find a word in Paragraph 1 that means *effect.*   _____

2. Find a word in Paragraph 5 that means *capable of being seen.*   _____

3. Find a word in Paragraph 12 that means *include.*   _____

4. Find a word in Paragraph 20 that means *expensive*. _____

5. Find a word in Paragraph 20 that means *decrease*. _____

✉ Translation

Translate the following sentences into Chinese.

1. The annual rates of 15 out of 24 major physical diseases were also significantly lower among those living closer to green spaces.

2. The health benefits for most of the diseases were only seen when the greenery was within a one kilometre (0. 62 miles) radius of the home.

3. The researchers also showed that this relation was strongest for children younger than 12.

4. They were 21% less likely to suffer from depression in the greener areas.

5. The researchers think the green spaces help recovery from stress and offer greater opportunities for social contacts.

✉ Cloze

Complete the following short passage by choosing proper words from the word bank provided.

protect	less	boosting	reducing	generally	difference	analysed	
unhealthy	suffer	Across	Under	extent	stop	fewest	regardless

A bit of greenery near our homes can cut the "health gap" between rich and poor, say researchers from two Scottish universities.

Even small parks in the heart of our cities can __1__ us from strokes and heart disease, perhaps by cutting stress or __2__ exercise.

Their study, in The Lancet, matched data about hundreds of thousands of deaths to green spaces in local areas.

Councils should introduce more greenery to improve wellbeing, they said.

__3__ the country, there are "health inequalities" related to income and social deprivation, which __4__ reflect differences in lifestyle, diet, and, to some __5__ , access to medical care.

This means that in general, people living in poorer areas are more likely to be

___6___ , and die earlier.

However, the researchers found that living near parks, woodland or other open spaces helped reduce these inequalities, ___7___ of social class.

When the records of more than 366,000 people who died between 2001 and 2005 were ___8___ , it revealed that even tiny green spaces in the areas in which they lived made a big ___9___ to their risk of fatal diseases.

Although the effect was greatest for those living surrounded by the most greenery, with the "health gap" roughly halved compared with those with the ___10___ green spaces around them, there was still a noticeable difference.

Discussion

Discuss the following questions with your class.

1. How do you think of green spaces in a residential area?
2. As college students, what do you think you should do to protect our environment?
3. Do you know any stories about someone who suffers from depression?
4. What ways shall we try to maintain our mental health?

■ Section B ■

To Cut Diabetes Heart Risks, Diet and Exercise May Beat Drugs

A 5-step action plan for lowering heart risks associated with diabetes

By Deborah Kotz

March 15, 2010

More than 1 in 10 American adults have diabetes, and many of them successfully keep their blood sugar levels under control with various medications. Unfortunately, these multibillion-dollar blockbuster drugs haven't proved to be so successful against the biggest cause of death related to diabetes: heart disease. Four new studies published in this week's *New England Journal of Medicine* bring nothing but disappointing news for diabetics who rely on drugs to lower their risk of heart attacks and strokes. One found that using antihypertensives to lower systolic (the top number) blood pressure below a healthful measurement of 120 mm Hg does nothing to lower a diabetic's risk of heart complications; another found no benefit to adding a drug to raise HDL "good" cholesterol levels in diabetics who were already taking a statin to lower the bad kind. And no heart benefits were associated with two drugs given to lower high blood sugar levels, according to the two other studies.

What all this new evidence suggests is that more may not always be better when it comes to finding ways to prevent heart disease in diabetics. "It's not enough to show that a drug lowers high blood sugar levels or other risky biomarkers," says Steven Nissen, chairman of the department of cardiovascular medicine at the Cleveland Clinic, whose research linked the diabetes drug Avandia with an increased rate of heart attacks. "Does it actually improve clinical outcomes? Does it cause more benefits than risks?"

Evidence is accumulating that diabetics may not benefit—and may even be worse off—when they're treated with medications to drive down their blood sugar levels or blood pressure to normal or below normal levels. The new study examining blood pressure found that diabetics with moderately high blood pressure levels—about 135 mm Hg on average—didn't benefit from taking extra blood pressure medication to lower those levels down to slightly less than 120 mm Hg. In fact, they were more likely than those who kept their levels in the 130s range to experience fainting, heart arrhythmias, and abnormally high potassium levels, all associated with low blood pressure. "Most doctors still aim for a goal blood pressure of 130 or below when treating diabetics, even though no there's no good data to support that," says study leader William Cushman, who is chief of preventive medicine at the VA Medical Center in Memphis. Still, he emphasizes, previous research has shown that diabetics can significantly lower their risk of heart attacks and strokes by getting treated with high blood pressure medications if they have a systolic blood pressure above 140 or a diastolic (lower number) pressure above 90.

The real take-home message here is that those with diabetes shouldn't forget about the importance of lifestyle factors even if they're already achieving optimal blood glucose levels with medications. "We have an abundance of evidence," says Cushman, that losing excess weight, increasing activity levels, and improving nutrition habits will lead to better control of diabetes and lower risks of heart disease. Plus, lifestyle modifications pose none of the side effects or long-term health risks that are associated with blood-sugar-lowering drugs. And these changes appear to be more effective than drugs like metformin at preventing diabetes from occurring in the first place in those who have prediabetes or insulin resistance, according to David Nathan, director of the diabetes Center at Massachusetts General Hospital, who wrote an editorial that accompanied two of the NEJM studies.

Here's a smart action plan:

1. Use drugs wisely. Those with diabetes should take a cholesterol-lowering statin drug to lower their heart-disease risks. They should take a blood pressure medication if they have a level above 140/90 mm Hg to reduce heart disease risks but shouldn't aim to achieve a level below 130 mm Hg for the systolic number, says Cushman. Glucose-lowering medications like metformin should be used to achieve a hemoglobin A1c level—a marker used to determine blood sugar control—of about 7. 5 percent. "Personally," he adds, "I'm concerned about driving levels below that with more medication because our previous research found a higher mortality rate in those who had levels as low as 6 percent. "

2. Think whole grains and whole foods. Following good nutrition habits is one of the best ways to control diabetes. You want to think high-quality carbohydrates like fruits, vegetables, and whole grains rather than highly processed foods (chips, pasta, cookies) that cause quick spikes in sugar levels. And you also want to include a lean protein choice (fish, tofu, turkey, or chicken breast) and a small amount of fat (nuts, olive oil, avocado) with every meal and snack to help slow digestion and keep sugar levels on an even keel.

3. Try the create-a-plate plan. Draw imaginary lines on your plate to divide it into three sections (two small, one large), then put salad greens, broccoli, or other nonstarchy vegetables onto the largest section of the plate; a small serving of starch (baked potato, rice, whole-wheat pasta) in one of the smaller sections, and a small serving of protein in the other.

4. Aim for modest weight loss. Most folks don't need to lose 40 or 50 pounds to help reverse diabetes. Just aiming for a 5 to 10 percent weight loss can make a huge difference in helping to control blood sugar levels, according to the American Diabetes Association.

5. Get moving, however you can. As with weight loss, you don't need to overdo it with the exercise to see some benefits. The biggest payoffs, in fact, come to those who are sedentary and simply get up and start walking around their neighborhood for 20 or 30 minutes a day, says John Morley, who is director of geriatrics at St. Louis University. "I literally write my patients a prescription to lift 5-pound weights in front of the TV or to always use the stairs instead of taking elevators or escalators," he says. "Every time they come in for a visit, I ask them if they're following my prescription, and I throw a tantrum if they're not. They actually respond to that."

http://www. usnews. com/health/managing-your-healthcare/diabetes/articles/2010/03/15/to-cut-diabetes-heart-risks-diet-and-exercise-may-beat-drugs. html?

Vocabulary

Match each word to its definition.

1. medication ( ) a. not up to expectations

2. blockbuster ( ) b. a drug that reduces high blood pressure

3. disappointing ( ) c. the act of treating with medicines or remedies

4. antihypertensive ( ) d. the most abundant steroid (类胆固醇) in animal tissues

5. systolic ( ) e. an unusually successful hit with widespread popularity and huge sales

6. complication ( ) f. of orrelating to a systole(心脏收缩) or happing during a systole

7. cholesterol ( ) g. an important source of physiological energy 葡萄糖

8. biomarker ( ) h. most desirable

9. cardiovascular ( ) i. any disease or disorder that occurs during the course of (or because of) another disease

10. glucose ( ) j. shaped and dried dough made from flour and water and sometimes egg(意大利面)

11. optimal ( ) k. another name for biological marker

12. tantrum   (   )   l. of or pertaining to or involving the heart and
                                    blood vessels

13. pasta   (   )   m. a display of bad temper

Discussion

Discuss the following questions with your class.

1. Do you know any tips that the patients should pay attention to when fighting against diabetes and heart disease?

2. What do you usually do to protect yourself from diseases?

3. Do you have the habit of conducting a physical examination of yourself?

4. How do you think the service provided in the hospitals of China nowadays?

Section C

Obama Signs Health Care Reform Bill, Aims to Promote It on the Road

March 23, 2010

Washington (CNN)—President Obama on Tuesday signed into law a sweeping health care reform bill, the nation's most substantial social legislation in four decades, achieving a top priority of his administration.

Greeted by applause from enthusiastic supporters, he said, "Today after almost a century of trying; today, after over a year of debate; today, after all the votes have been tallied, health insurance reform becomes law in the United States of America."

The president said he is confident the Senate will improve the health care reform law swiftly. He said some health care reforms will take some time to phase in, but others will "take effect right away."

Obama introduced the widow of the late Sen. Ted Kennedy, who championed health care reform. "It's fitting that Ted's widow Vicki is here, and his niece, Caroline, his son, Patrick, whose vote helped make this health care reform a reality." Patrick Kennedy is a congressman from Rhode Island.

Obama said Tuesday that under provisions of the health care legislation that will take effect this year, small businesses will receive tax credits to help cover insurance, insurance companies won't be able to drop people's coverage when they get sick, and uninsured Americans and parents of children with pre-existing conditions will be able to purchase coverage.

He said he signed the bill into law on behalf of several people, including his mother, "who argued with insurance companies even as she battled cancer in her final days." He praised Senate Majority Leader Harry Reid, House Speaker Nancy Pelosi and congressional committee chairs, saying, "We are blessed by leaders in each chamber who not only do their jobs very well, but who never lost sight of the larger mission. They didn't play for the short term. They didn't play to the polls or the politics."

"We are not a nation that scales back its aspirations," the president said. "We are not a nation that falls prey to doubt or mistrust. We don't fall prey to fear. We are not a nation that does what's easy. It's not who we are. It's not how we got here. We are a nation that faces its challenges and accepts its responsibilities."

Before the signing, Vice President Joe Biden, praising Obama's leadership in forging the legislation, said, "Mr. President, you've done what generations of not just ordinary, but great men and women have attempted to do... You delivered on a promise, a promise you made to all Americans when we moved into this building," the White House.

Obama will hit the road to sell the measure to a still-skeptical public, giving a speech Thursday in Iowa City, Iowa, White House press secretary Robert Gibbs said. Obama launched his grass-roots drive for health care reform in Iowa City in May 2007, according to Gibbs.

The bill passed the House of Representatives late Sunday night with no Republican support. It was approved by the Senate in December.

A separate compromise package of changes also passed the House on Sunday and still needs to be approved by the Senate. The officials noted that the Senate cannot begin debate on the package before Obama signs the underlying bill into law.

What will health care reform mean to you?

Passage of the bill was a huge boost for Obama. Aides said Monday that Obama exchanged handshakes, hugs and "high-fives" with staffers when the outcome of the House vote became apparent.

"I haven't seen the president so happy about anything other than his family since I've known him," said senior adviser David Axelrod, adding that Obama's jubilation Sunday night exceeded his election victory in November 2008. "He was excited that night, but not like last night."

Republicans promised to continue fighting the reforms, with 11 state attorneys general—all Republican—planning lawsuits challenging the constitutionality of the bill's mandate for people to buy health insurance and requirements for states to comply with its provisions.

Senior Republicans in Congress warned that voters will judge Democrats harshly in November's midterm elections, with Sen. John McCain of Arizona saying the Democratic-passed bill killed any chance of bipartisan support on legislation for the rest of the year.

"There will be no cooperation for the rest of this year," McCain said in an interview with KFYI radio in Arizona. "They have poisoned the well in what they have done and how they have done it."

Gibbs, however, said the administration expects to win any lawsuits filed against the bill, and he challenged McCain and other Republicans to campaign for the November election against benefits of the health care bill such as tax credits for small businesses and an end to insurance company practices such as denying coverage for pre-existing conditions.

The overall $ 940 billion plan is projected to extend insurance coverage to roughly 32 million additional Americans.

Most Americans will now be required to have health insurance or pay a fine. Larger employers will be required to provide coverage or risk financial penalties. Lifetime coverage limits will be banned, and insurers will be barred from denying coverage based on gender or pre-existing conditions.

The compromise package would add to the bill's total cost partly by expanding insurance subsidies for middle-and lower-income families. The measure would scale back the bill's taxes on expensive insurance plans.

House Democrats are expected to celebrate passage of the bill at a news conference with reform advocates Tuesday afternoon. Secretary of State Hillary Clinton, who spearheaded her husband's failed health reform effort in the 1990s, said earlier in the day that Obama's success was an example of the president's tenacity.

"If you ever doubt the resolve of President Obama to stay with a job, look at what we got done for the United States last night when it came to passing quality affordable health care for everyone," Clinton said during a speech to the American Israel Public Affairs Committee.

Observers warn, however, that the road ahead for health care reform in the Senate may be rocky. Democratic leaders are using a legislative maneuver called reconciliation, which will allow the compromise plan to clear the Senate with a simple majority of 51 votes. But according to Senate rules, members are still allowed to offer unlimited amendments and challenges.

In one of the first of many attempts Republicans say they will make to try to amend or kill the package, GOP aides went to Senate Parliamentarian Alan Frumin on Monday to argue that the compromise bill violates rules of the reconciliation process because of the way it affects Social Security. For that reason, GOP aides said they argued, the bill should not even be allowed to be debated.

However, Frumin, according to a senior Republican and a Democratic aide, informed both parties he disagreed with the GOP assessment, and would not block the bill from reaching the Senate floor.

"There's hope that [the vote] would be done within a short period of time, like a week or so," said Tim McBride, a health economist and associate dean of public health at the Brown School at Washington University in St. Louis, Missouri.

"But the Senate is complicated and doesn't have the discipline that the House does."

Once the package hits the Senate floor, the chamber's rules stipulate that there must be 20 hours of debate. But that 20 hours may prove to be more of a suggestion than an indicator of what will happen, according to Cheryl Block, a law professor at Washington University's School of Law.

"It could get all messy and could go on forever if [Republicans] threw up amendment after amendment," Block said.

"Theoretically, it should only take 20 hours, but it will likely take longer because Republicans have things up their sleeve. "

If any provision in the package of changes is rejected or changed, the entire package would then have to go back to the House for another vote.

House Democrats unhappy with the Senate bill have been continually reassured that the compromise package will be approved by the more conservative Senate.

Senate Majority Leader Harry Reid, D-Nevada, presented a letter to House Democrats on Saturday stating that their Senate counterparts "believe that health insurance reform cannot wait and must not be obstructed. "

So far, two of the 59 senators in the Democratic caucus, Ben Nelson of Nebraska and Blanche Lincoln of Arkansas, have said they will oppose the compromise package.

http://www. antiguaobserver. com/? p = 27778

Discussion

Discuss the following questions with your class.

1. How do you think the health care system in China now?

2. Do you know some health care systems of foreign counties?

3. Can you list some other reforms pushed ahead with by Obama since his assumption?

4. What does the health care system mean to you and to a country?

Unit Six

Economy

Section A

Europe's Debt Crisis: What It Means for Americans

The Issue in the News

The Greek government has spent too much for years. Markets became concerned about this in November after the newly elected Socialist government revealed that last year's budget deficit was more than three times as large as previously estimated. The EU says Greece's financial figures have been fudged for years.

With debt piling up to 113% of the economy, investors fear Greece won't pay its debts, in the form of government bonds—or will need a lifeline from other EU countries to meet its 54 billion euro ($ 74 billion) borrowing needs this year.

Greece's debt crisis has global implications because it's the most visible example of the massive build-up in public deficits around the world after governments loosened the purse strings to mitigate the global credit crunch.

That means governments have to cut spending, raise taxes and divert revenues to pay off interest on their debts.

Furthermore, because of the worries that Greece may default, investors are demanding higher interest payments before they will lend any more money. The risk premium raises rates on assets, such as corporate bonds— meaning companies themselves find it more expensive to borrow.

Points to Notice

As you read, pay attention to the following facets and information mentioned in this piece of news:

- Greek financial woes
- European Union
- Major countries involved in this debt crisis
- Two ways the crisis could affect the U.S.
- Market psychology

Text

by Corey Flintoff

February 11, 2010

The debt crisis in Greece[1] may seem remote to Americans, but experts say it could impact the financial recovery for the U.S. and the world.

The Greek financial woes were a top priority Thursday at a summit of European leaders seeking to calm fears over the debt problems in the euro zone, the 16 EU nations where the euro is the common currency.

Greece uses the euro, and investors' confidence in that normally strong currency has been shaken by the prospect that Athens could default on its debts. Europeans leaders, led by France and Germany, have agreed to a plan to come to the aid of Greece in an effort to quell concerns over the long-term health of the European economy.

European Union President Herman Van Rompuy told reporters in Brussels that the Greek government hasn't requested any financial support, but that euro zone members are ready to take coordinated action, if necessary, to protect their financial stability.

Top European leaders, including French President Nicholas Sarkozy and German Chancellor Angela Merkel, met with Greek Prime Minister George Papandreou to discuss Greece's plan for cutting its deficit over several years.

The Greek crisis has contributed to the general air of uncertainty in international financial markets, says economist Joseph Stiglitz. Greece is one of five euro zone countries now struggling with big national debts.

Major Implications

"The major implications are for Greece, Spain, Portugal, Italy and Ireland and therefore in some sense for all of Europe," says Stiglitz, a Nobel Prize-winning economist at Columbia University.

The problems in the euro zone could impact the U. S. , too, Stiglitz says, especially if they dampen sales of U. S. exports to Europe.

The crisis began after last year's elections, when the new government discovered Greece was breaking euro zone rules that say a member country's debt must not exceed 3 percent of its gross domestic product. Greece's debt was a whopping 12. 7 percent of GDP, and the new Greek government ministers claimed their predecessors had been lying about it.

The value of the euro has dropped against the dollar as the Greek crisis unfolded, from an average of $ 1. 49 to the euro last November to around $ 1. 38 on Wednesday. It has stabilized somewhat as currency markets saw signs that euro zone governments, led by Germany and France, were putting together an aid package that would help the Greek government avoid default.

Stiglitz stresses that he's not a doomsayer, and says he doesn't think Greece is in danger of defaulting on its debt. But, he says, there are two ways that the uncertainty over the crisis could affect the U. S.

One way America will be affected, Stiglitz says, is that the crisis is putting more pressure on countries all over the world to engage in deficit reduction. That means lower aggregate demand for goods and services of all kinds, including American goods and services, he says.

"One of the things we've been counting on to help our recovery is exports," Stiglitz says, and the crisis could affect exports in another way as well. If the euro weakens in relation to the dollar, U. S. goods will become far more expensive for Europeans, who likely will buy less.

Market Psychology

Sebastian Mallaby, an economist at the Council on Foreign Relations, says he doesn't see any real threat to U. S. exports yet, but there is always a danger that market psychology could be undermined.

"Greece—here's a government that had way too much debt and now can't pay creditors. Can you think of any other governments that could be in the same position?" he asks.

That could describe the situation of many governments, including the U. S. But for now, the focus is on the euro zone countries that have come to be known as PIIGS, for Portugal, Italy, Ireland, Greece and Spain.

They are the countries where austerity measures are likely to bite the hardest, and where appetites for imported goods are likely to dry up.

So far, many American companies selling abroad are reluctant to make public predictions about what European markets may be like for them in the immediate future.

Caterpillar[2], the nation's biggest exporter of heavy equipment, declined to comment for this article. A company spokesman said it's too early to determine whether the European debt crisis will affect Caterpillar's business.

Joseph Dehner, an international business lawyer, says it has been easier in recent months to promote U. S. exports while the value of the euro was high in relation to the dollar.

Dehner is chairman of the international services group at Frost Brown Todd, a Louisville, Ky. -based law firm that advises several big U. S. companies that do business in Europe, including Ford[3] and General Electric[4].

The debt crisis and confidence in the euro aren't real issues yet, he says, "but if this lasts for a few months, it will definitely be a big problem."

http://www. npr. org/templates/story/story. php? storyId = 123603449

Online Resources

http://www. theglobeandmail. com/report-on-business/economy/europes-debt-crisis-threat-to-recovery/article1456804/

http://www. guardian. co. uk/business/interactive/2010/apr/28/europe-economy-dominoes-greece-eu

http://www. washingtonpost. com/wp-dyn/content/article/2010/05/07/AR20100 50703436. html

http://www. usatoday. com/money/economy/2010-02-05-q-and-a-europe-debt _ N. htm

Vocabulary

1.	woes	*n.*	the problems and troubles affecting someone 不幸,困难
2.	currency	*n.*	the metal or paper medium of exchange that is presently used 货币;流通
3.	default	*n. /vi.*	act of failing to meet a financial obligation 拖欠
4.	quell	*vt.*	overcome 平息,镇定
5.	stability	*n.*	a stable order 稳定性
6.	dampen	*vt.*	make something such as an activity less strong:使沮丧,泼凉水
7.	exceed	*vt. /vi.*	to be more than a particular number or amount 超出,超过
8.	whopping	*adj.*	very large 巨大的,天大的
9.	predecessor	*n.*	one who precedes you in time (as in holding a position or

office)前辈,前任

10. doomsayer *n.* someone who says that bad things are going to happen 凶事预示者

11. aggregate *adj.* the whole amount of 合计的,集合的

12. austerity *n.* bad economic conditions in which people do not have much money to spend

13. prediction *n.* a statement made about the future 预言,预测

Language Notes

1. **Greece**: a country in southeastern Europe, situated on the southern end of the Balkan Peninsula. By the end of 2009, as a result of a combination of international (financial crisis) and local factors, the Greek economy faced its most severe crisis since 1993.

2. **Caterpillar Inc.**, also known as "CAT", designs, manufactures, markets and sells machinery and engines and sells financial products and insurance to customers via a worldwide dealer network.. Caterpillar is the world's largest manufacturer of construction and mining equipment, diesel and natural gas engines and industrial gas turbines. With more than USD $ 67 billion in assets, Caterpillar was ranked number one in its industry and number 44 overall in the 2009 Fortune 500. Caterpillar stock is a component of the Dow Jones Industrial Average.

3. The **Ford Motor Company**: an American multinational corporation based in Dearborn, Michigan, a suburb of Detroit. The automaker was founded by Henry Ford and incorporated on June 16, 1903. Ford is currently the second largest automaker in the U. S. and the fourth-largest in the world based on number of vehicles sold annually, directly behind Volkswagen.

4. The **General Electric Company**, **or GE**: an American multinational conglomerate corporation incorporated in the State of New York. In 2010, Forbes ranked GE as the world's second largest company. The company has 304,000 employees around the world.

Exercises

✉ Vocabulary and Expressions

A. Idioms and Expressions

Fill in the blanks with the correct idiom or expression.

1. count on someone or something：to rely on someone or something；to depend on someone or something 指望某人/某事物

Can I count on this car to start every morning of the year?

2. dry up：to disappear or end（使）枯竭，消失

Funding has all but dried up for new research in the field.

3. put together：to create by putting components or members together 合在一起

Ministers are trying to put together a package that will end the dispute.

1. When I _____ all the facts, I found the answer.

2. We can _____ Bill to get the job done.

3. Many of those jobs _____ in the 1990s.

B. Vocabulary

Fill in the blanks with the words given below. Change the form where necessary.

> woes currency default prediction quell stability dampen
> exceed whopping predecessor doomsayer aggregate austerity

1. The company is in _____ on its loan agreement.

2. The light rain _____ the crowd's enthusiasm.

3. The country is experiencing great economic _____ .

4. Our new doctor is much younger than his _____ .

5. There are _____ restrictions on the sums allowed for foreign travel.

6. _____ money is spent on advertisements every year.

7. The government's reassurances have done nothing to _____ the doubts of

the public.

8. The data can be used to make useful economic _____.

9. It could threaten the peace and _____ of the region.

10. His performance _____ our expectations.

✉ Exploring Content

A. Complete the sentences based on the reading text.

1. At a summit of European leaders gave priority to the Greek financial woes seeking to _____ in the euro zone.

2. The prospect that Athens could fail to repay its debts has shaken investors' confidence in _____.

3. Greece was discovered breaking euro zone rules that say a member country's debt must not exceed _____, which caused the crisis.

4. Stiglitz says, One way America will be affected, is that the crisis is putting more pressure on countries all over the world to engage in _____.

5. So far, many American companies selling abroad are reluctant to _____ about what European markets may be like for them in the immediate future.

B. Match the following people on the left to their statements on the right.

1. Europeans leaders

 a. U. S. exports have not been threatened yet, but there is always a danger that market psychology could be undermined.

2. Herman Van Rompuy

 b. It has been easier in recent months to promote U. S. exports while the value of the euro was high in relation to the dollar.

3. Joseph Stiglitz

 c. The Greek government hasn't requested any financial support, but that euro zone members are ready to help.

4. Sebastian Mallaby

 d. Exports is one of the things that is expected to help Greece recovery, and the crisis could affect exports in another way as well.

5. Joseph Dehner

 e. A plan to come to the aid of Greece has been

agreed in an effort to overcome worries over the long-term health of the European economy.

 **Translation**

Translate the following sentences into Chinese.

1. The debt crisis in Greece may seem remote to Americans, but experts say it could impact the financial recovery for the U. S. and the world.

2. Top European leaders, including French President Nicholas Sarkozy and German Chancellor Angela Merkel, met with Greek Prime Minister George Papandreou to discuss Greece's plan for cutting its deficit over several years.

3. The value of the euro has dropped against the dollar as the Greek crisis unfolded, from an average of $ 1.49 to the euro last November to around $ 1.38 on Wednesday.

4. If the euro weakens in relation to the dollar, U. S. goods will become far more expensive for Europeans, who likely will buy less.

5. A company spokesman said it's too early to determine whether the European debt crisis will affect Caterpillar's business.

Cloze

Complete the following short passage by choosing proper words from the word bank provided.

boom transaction worst setback comparatively counterparts Asian
European preparing selling buying anxieties fallen risen remain

Anxiety about Europe's debt crisis last month caused U. S. stocks to suffer their __1__ month in more than a year. Yet many experts say fears that Europe will deal a sharp __2__ to the U. S. economy are overblown.

They note that trade between the U. S. and Europe is __3__ small. U. S. banks do lend to their European __4__ and hold billions in investments in those banks and other European firms. But U. S. banks have enough capital to withstand losses from a __5__ crisis, analysts say.

In addition, the European Union is __6__ a $ 1 trillion bailout for weak member-states. And its central bank has begun __7__ government debt to protect European banks—and their U. S. counterparts—from the risk of default by EU countries.

The __8__ that have spooked U. S. stock markets could linger a while. The Dow Jones industrial average has __9__ more than 12 percent since late April. But the foundations of the U. S. economy __10__ secure, experts say.

"The physical linkages with Europe just aren't big enough to undercut the U. S. economy," said Ethan Harris, head of North American economics at Bank of America Merrill Lynch.

Discussion

Discuss the following questions with your class.

1. Can you name the member countries of Euro zone?
2. What do you know of Greece?
3. What are the influences of Europe's debt crisis on Chinese market in your view?
4. What are the function of the European Union in Europe and the world?

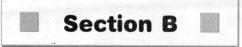

Section B

Davos 2010: The West Accepts India and China as Equals

By Tim Weber

Business editor, BBC News website, in Davos

28 January 2010

Once again, China and India are high on the agenda at the World Economic Forum.

But something is different. Once they were seen as promising markets—China as workbench and India as services provider—for Western companies.

The past 18 months have changed all that.

At long last, both countries—and other emerging markets like Brazil—are being accepted as true equals.

What a difference a global financial crisis can make.

'China-centric world'

In previous years, Chinese and Indian executives tended to display a prickly nationalism. Speaking to them, I always had the feeling that they tried to prove their importance.

Not anymore.

"Post-meltdown, post-recession, there's a positively different expectation of India," says Anand Mahindra, managing director of automotive group Mahindra and Mahindra.

The power shift is raising expectations.

"India wants to be part of the spec sheet. Are we there when the terms are being set for any major global issue?" asks Mr Mahindra.

In one of the meeting rooms here in Davos, a wall is dominated by a stylised map of the world. It's a look from high above the south pole. Latin America, Africa and Asia loom large.

The US and Western Europe look rather puny. And the UK is a mere speck on the wall.

Once, "the United States could export its recession around the world," says Stephen King, the group chief economist of HSBC bank.

This crisis is different. Emerging economies, especially China and India, managed to avoid the worst of the contagion.

It's "not perfect decoupling," says Mr King, but over the long-term the crisis has sown the seeds for a move towards a "China-centric world rather than a US centric world".

New trading bloc

Stuart Gulliver, executive director at HSBC, sees a new economic bloc emerging that would sideline the US and Western Europe—stretching from China, Asia Pacific, the Middle East and Africa to Latin America.

As a bloc, these countries have "a lot of investable capital, huge commodity wealth, huge production capital and huge demand".

It's an area of emerging countries with so much domestic demand that a crisis in the West may cause it to stutter, but not to grind to a halt, argues Mr Gulliver.

Mr King points to the last three months of 2009, when China's economy (and its exports) rebounded, even when US consumer demand did not.

The crisis has tipped the power balance.

This makes emerging economies a great place to invest, say private-equity investors like David Rubenstein of the Carlyle Group.

Sir Martin Sorrell, chief executive of advertising group WPP, says that if you're running a global company, "there's no choice, you have to build your operations in these high-growth areas."

China versus India?

But it is here, he says, where China has the edge.

"Without infrastructure it won't work. And that's the big difference between India and China."

Speak to any corporate boss from India, and they will admit that infrastructure problems—and bureaucracy—are holding the country back.

Take Priya Hiranandani-Vandrevala, the chief executive of Hirco, India's largest residential property developer.

Her company builds homes for the emerging middle classes—developments of 10,000 units for 50,000 people—schools, hospitals and sewage plants included.

Getting such a project built can take eight to 12 years, she says, and requires a lot of work.

India's infrastructure is "frightfully underdeveloped," she says, and it is little surprise that "India has the third-lowest cement demand per capita in the world".

But her industry also demonstrates how India's economy is changing.

When the recession struck, the Indian real estate market "completely shut down for three to five months at the beginning of 2009," she says.

Then demand picked up sharply again—driven not by buyers working for Western companies but by truly domestic demand.

After all, according to Rajat Gupta of consulting firm McKinsey, India has the potential for the largest middle class in the world.

India is a country that is turning "one billion people into one billion consumers," says Manvinder Banga, the president of Unilever's global food and personal care division.

It will be these consumers, that will truly shift the world's economic power balance. Maybe not this decade.

But if Davos is any guide, it won't take much longer.

http://news.bbc.co.uk/2/hi/business/8486094.stm

Vocabulary

Match each word to its definition.

1. workbench	( )	a.	a situation in which prices fall by a very large amount or an industry or economic situation becomes much weaker
2. prickly	( )	b.	abbr. a detailed instruction about how a building, car, piece of equipment etc should be made [= specification]
3. nationalism	( )	c.	inferior in strength or significance
4. meltdown	( )	d.	causing a lot of disagreements and difficulties
5. spec	( )	e.	strong table used for working on with tools
6. stylised	( )	f.	a strong feeling attacheel to a nation or nationality
7. puny	( )	g.	a situation in which a disease is spread
8. speck	( )	h.	using artistic forms and conventions to create effects
9. contagion	( )	i.	a large group of people or countries with the same political aims, working together
10. bloc	( )	j.	very small mark, spot, or piece of something
11. sideline	( )	k.	a stop or pause
12. stutter	( )	l.	a complicated official system
13. halt	( )	m.	waste matter carried away in sewers or drains
14. tip	( )	n.	concrete pavement
15. bureaucracy	( )	o.	remove from the center of activity or attention
16. sewage	( )	p.	to speak with difficulty because you cannot stop yourself from repeating some words
17. per capita	( )	q.	move into a sloping position, so that one end or side is higher than the other
18. cement	( )	r.	per person

Discussion

Discuss the following questions with your class.

1. What do you know of India?

2. Do you think China and India can be good friends and neighbors in the future?

3. Do you believe the world will become a "China-centric world" one day?

4. How do you think China should do to keep friendly relationship with her neighbors?

■ Section C ■

Global Economic Crisis Abated, but Effects Linger

by Tom Gjelten

January 2, 2010

One year can make a big difference. In January 2009, global unemployment was soaring, the international financial system was in near-meltdown, world trade was in free fall, and economists were warning that a turnaround was not in sight. Governments faced the prospect of widespread social instability and popular unrest, and historians were recalling that the Great Depression set the stage for World War II. In February, the director of national intelligence, Dennis Blair, told the U.S. Congress that the global economic crisis had replaced terrorism as "the primary near-term security concern of the United States."

Since then, international stock markets have rebounded, unemployment rates have leveled off, world trade has picked up and the global economy is growing again. On Christmas Day, an apparent al-Qaida attempt to blow up a Northwest Airlines jet in flight reminded Americans that terrorist attacks were still a danger. Intelligence officials are no longer describing global economic problems as the paramount U.S. security concern.

Economic recovery, however, has been anemic in many countries, and the global recession has had repercussions that are likely to be felt for a long time. The events of the past year and a half have reshaped the world economy, left governments and bankers with new worries and altered the geopolitical landscape. The once-dominant Group of 7 industrial countries, including the United States, Japan and European powers, has largely been eclipsed, with emerging economies now poised to play leadership roles that were unimaginable just a few years ago.

The big winner in 2009 was clearly China, with its global economic position actually strengthening as a result of the crisis. Spurred by an early and bold government stimulus program, the Chinese economy was growing at nearly a 9 percent annual rate by the end of the third quarter, with the prospect of even faster growth ahead. The State Council for Development Research Center, a government think tank in Beijing, has just predicted a 9. 5 percent growth rate for 2010. At that rate, China could soon have the second-biggest national economy in the world, replacing Japan, which is still struggling in its return to growth.

Brazil has also become a superstar performer, with stock values there surging more than 80 percent in 2009. European countries, meanwhile, have lagged far behind. Germany is prospering, but Portugal, Italy, Ireland, Greece and Spain share such severe problems that they have been given a new name: They now constitute the "PIIGS." Even Britain, a pillar of the European economy, was still in recession at the end of the third quarter.

"The old distinction between safe and unsafe markets has been turned on its head," says David Gordon, head of global research for the Eurasia Group. "The mature markets have for years been seen as less risky than emerging markets. But the big problems in the European countries are reversing that."

The political consequences of the economic shift could be far-reaching. One lesson of the climate change conference in Copenhagen was that China now outweighs Europe in diplomatic clout. But its rising economic power could prompt governments to take a harder line with Beijing in regard to trade, investment and exchange rate issues, with the prospect of increasing conflict rather than growing cooperation.

One example: the U. S. International Trade Commission in December sided with U. S. steelmakers and imposed new duties on imports of subsidized Chinese steel.

Brazil, meanwhile, is moving toward a more nationalist stance in the protection of its abundant energy resources.

New Economic Challenges Still Emerging

The development of a more multipolar world could lead to greater international collaboration if it is accompanied by the strengthening of international institutions such as the United Nations, the World Bank and the International Monetary Fund. So far, however, the record is mixed. While the IMF has taken a bigger role in the management of the global economy, the United Nations and the World Bank, if anything, saw their prestige diminished with the failure of the Copenhagen conference to produce a binding climate agreement.

Finally, while the global financial crisis has abated, new economic challenges are still emerging. One concern is the growing seriousness of sovereign debt, which is debt owed by governments rather than private companies or financial institutions. Banks have traditionally seen government bonds as essentially risk-free, meaning that the prospect of defaulting on repayment has been considered remote. But Dubai frightened investors with its failure to meet a debt payment in November, and the Greek government recently saw its bond rating slip as a result of its severe fiscal problems. One consequence may be that banks will need to set aside larger capital reserves to protect against the risk of government default, and that could adversely affect private lending and jeopardize growth.

Still, the big economic story of the past year may be what did not happen. The Great Recession of 2008-2009 did not lead to another Great Depression. Arvind Subramanian, a senior fellow at the Peterson Institute of International Economics in Washington, wrote recently in the Financial Times newspaper that governments in 2009 showed that they had learned what would not work: overly tight monetary or fiscal policies and beggar-thy-neighbor protectionist measures. "The impact of this global financial crisis has been significantly limited," Subramanian wrote, "because on each of these scores, the policy mistakes of the past were strenuously and knowingly avoided."

International economic developments are still being closely monitored by U. S. intelligence analysis, but the worries that propelled the global economy to the forefront of U. S. security concerns just a year ago do seem to have diminished.

http://www. npr. org/templates/story/story. php? storyId = 122155918

Discussion

Discuss the following questions with your class.

1. Can you share what you know about the current situation of the job market in China with your friends?

2. How do you regard the impact from the global financial crisis and Europe's debt crisis on China?

3. What do you know of Brazil, especially in the economic area?

4. Do you agree that international economic developments are being controlled by the Wall Street?

Unit Seven

Society and Life

Section A

Apple Boss Defends Conditions at iPhone Factory

"You go in this place and it's a factory but, my gosh, they've got restaurants and movie theatres and hospitals and swimming pools"

——Steve Jobs Apple CEO

The Issue in the News

The Foxconn factory in Longhua in the southern Guangdong province, which makes iPods, iPads and iPhones among other devices, has seen 16 suicides this year. The latest death happened just hours after Foxconn chief executive Terry Gou, one of Taiwan's most famous businessmen, had taken international media on a tour of the plant and assured hundreds of reporters that the plant was under control.

An undercover team of seven Chinese investigators infiltrated the

Longhua plant. The Organizer Zhu Guangbing revealed, "The facilities at Foxconn are fine, but the management is poor. Hundreds of people work in the workshops but they are not allowed to talk to each other." He said Foxconn had lost tens of thousands of workers during the financial crisis and had been stretched to the breaking point by the volume of new orders.

HP, Apple and Dell have all released statements offering condolences and say they will investigate working conditions at the plant. "Any reports of poor working conditions in Dell's supply chain are investigated and, if warranted, appropriate action is taken," Sharon Zhang, a spokeswoman for Dell, told Agence France-Presse. "We expect our suppliers to employ the same high standards as we do in our own facilities."

Points to Notice

As you may read, pay attention to the following facets and information mentioned in this piece of news:

● Foxconn worker suicides

● Counter-measure: a 20% pay increase to workers

● Apple boss Jobs's defence for Foxconn

● Jobs' response to the dispute between Apple and Adobe over the Flash platform

Text

2 June 2010

Apple boss Steve Jobs has defended conditions at a Taiwanese electronics firm that produces the firm's popular iPhone, following a spate of suicides.

"Foxconn[1] is not a sweatshop," he told a conference in the US.

Mr Jobs said that Apple representatives were working with Foxconn to find out why 10 workers had killed themselves at a factory in Shenzhen, China.

An eleventh worker recently died at another factory in northern China.

In total, there have been 13 suicides and suicide attempts at Foxconn factories this year.

"We're all over this," said Mr Jobs at the All Things Digital conference in California.

Foxconn has said that it will give its assembly line workers a 30% pay rise.

The firm had previously said that it would offer a 20% pay increase to its Chinese workers, who earn 900 yuan (£ 90) per month at entry-level.

"We hope the hike in wages will help improve the living standards of the workers and allow them to have more leisure time, which is good for their health," an official of Foxconn's parent company Hon Hai precision told AFP.

Hon Hai Precision is the world's largest maker of consumer electronics, and employs 800,000 workers worldwide, mostly in China.

Foxconn makes a range of products for manufacturers including Apple, Dell and Nokia.

The deaths have shone a spotlight on working conditions at the factory, where workers—often from rural China—work up to 12 hours a day, six days a week.

But Mr Jobs defended the conditions.

"You go in this place and it's a factory but, my gosh, they've got restaurants and movie theatres and hospitals and swimming pools. For a factory, it's pretty nice," he said.

Surreal moment

Mr Jobs addressed a number of other issues at the All Things Digital conference.

Last week, Apple overtook Microsoft to become the world's largest technology company by market value.

"For those of us that have been in the industry a long time, it's surreal. But it doesn't matter very much, it's not what's important," Mr Jobs said.

"It's not what makes you come to work every morning."

He also claimed that Apple's controversial move to block Adobe Flash[2] animation and video technology from its popular iPhones and iPads was "a technical decision".

"We didn't start off to have a war with Flash or anything else," he said.

The comments are the latest step in a long-running dispute between Apple and Adobe over the Flash platform.

http://news. bbc. co. uk/2/hi/technology/10212604. stm

Vocabulary

1.	spate	*n.*	a sudden or strong outburst; a large number or amount
2.	suicide	*vi.*	to put (oneself) to death
3.	sweatshop	*n.*	a shop or factory in which employees work for long hours at low wages and under unhealthy conditions
4.	representative	*n.*	a typical example of a group, class, or quality
5.	previously	*adv.*	going before in time or order
6.	hike	*n.*	an increase especially in quantity or amount
7.	standard	*n.*	something established by authority, custom, or general consent as a model or example
8.	precision	*n.*	the quality of being very exact or correct
9.	range	*n.*	a number of people or things that are all different, but are all of the same general type
10.	spotlight	*n.*	conspicuous public notice
11.	surreal	*adj.*	marked by the intense irrational reality of a dream
12.	overtook	*vt.*	to develop or increase more quickly than someone or something else and become more successful, more important, or more advanced than them
13.	controversial	*adj.*	causing a lot of disagreement, because many people have strong opinions about the subject being discussed
14.	animation	*n.*	the process of making animated films, television programmes, computer games

15. comment   *n.*   an observation or remark expressing an opinion or attitude

Language Notes

1. **Foxconn**: a Taiwan-registered corporation headquartered in Tucheng, Taiwan, is the largest manufacturer of electronics and computer components worldwide and mainly manufactures on contract to other companies

2. **Adobe Flash** (formerly Macromedia Flash): a proprietary multimedia platform used to add animation, video, and interactivity to Web pages. Flash is frequently used for advertisements and games. More recently, it has been positioned as a tool for "Rich Internet Applications" ("RIAs").

Exercises

 Vocabulary and Expressions

A. Idioms and Expressions

Fill in the blanks with the correct idiom or expression.

1. **a spate of**: a large number of similar things that happen in a short period of time, especially bad things 大量的

A spate of burglaries keeps on happening in this area.

2. **in total**: the whole number of something 总共

This product will cost you 50 pounds in total.

3. **a range of**: a number of people or things that are all different, but are all of the same general type 一套,一系列

It's an electric drill with a range of different attachments.

1. The number of students who are absent today is 23 _____.

2. There is _____ murder happening in the town.

3. The drug is effective against _____ bacteria.

B. Vocabulary

Fill in the blanks with the words given below. Change the form where necessary.

| sweatshop overtake standard controversial range |
| previously suicide spotlight comment spate |

1. There is no absolute _____ for beauty.

2. He committed _____ during a fit of depression.

3. The land _____ cultivated returned to forest.

4. Television soon _____ the cinema as the most popular form of entertainment.

5. He spent three years in a _____ before he found a decent job.

6. In recent years economic growth has become a _____ goal.

7. America has produced a _____ of musical plays that have been phenomenally popular abroad as well as at home.

8. The minister refused to _____ on the rumors of his resignation.

9. Several cars are available within this price _____ .

10. There are many _____ on the stage.

Exploring Content

A. Complete the sentences based on the reading text.

1. Apple boss Steve Jobs told a conference in the US that _____ .

2. Foxconn has said that _____ .

3. The firm had previously said that it would offer a 20% pay increase to its Chinese workers, _____ .

4. We hope the hike in wages will help improve the living standards of the workers and _____ .

5. Last week, Apple overtook Microsoft to _____ .

B. Put a check(✓) next to the statements that the writer would agree with.

1. ( ) An eleventh worker recently died in the same factory of China.

2. ( ) In total, there have been 13 suicides and suicide attempts at Foxconn factories in recent years.

3. ( ) Foxconn has said that it will give all the workers a 30% pay rise.

4. ( ) The deaths have shone a spotlight on working conditions at the factory, where workers—often from rural China—work up to more than 12 hours a day, six days a week.

5. ( ) The comments are the latest step in a long-running dispute between Apple and Adobe over the Flash platform.

6. ( ) Mr. Jobs claimed that Apple's controversial move to block Adobe Flash animation and video technology from its popular iPhones and iPads was "a technical decision".

 Translation

Translate the following sentences into Chinese.

1. In total, there have been 13 suicides and suicide attempts at Foxconn factories this year.

2. The firm had previously said that it would offer a 20% pay increase to its Chinese workers, who earn 900 yuan (£ 90) per month at entry-level.

3. The deaths have shone a spotlight on working conditions at the factory, where workers—often from rural China—work up to 12 hours a day, six days a week.

4. Last week, Apple overtook Microsoft to become the world's largest technology company by market value.

5. He also claimed that Apple's controversial move to block Adobe Flash animation and video technology from its popular iPhones and iPads was "a technical decision".

 Cloze

Complete the following short passage by choosing proper words from the word bank provided.

changed	doubtfully	commit	awkward	devices	impetus	radical	
incur	twisted	clumsy	reckless	survived	calm	trigger	allegedly

While Apple has risen to become the world's largest technology firm, Foxconn, the maker of almost all of its __1__ , appears to have broken under the pressure of keeping up with new orders.

Two more workers attempted to __2__ suicide on Thursday by jumping from the top of dormitory buildings at its giant Longhua factory, according to sources at the site. Both __3__ and are currently hospitalised.

So far, at least 16 people have jumped from high buildings at the factory so far this year, with 12 deaths.

The hysteria at Longhua, where between 300,000 and 400,000 employees eat, work and sleep, has grown to such a pitch that workers have __4__ Foxconn's Chinese name so that it now sounds like: "Run to your Death".

Terry Gou, the 59-year-old billionaire who founded the company, in a meeting with his senior management, __5__ said that he would not now leave the factory until the suicides stop.

In addition, the company is said to be considering a __6__ plan to move 60,000 people, or 20pc of its workforce at Longhua, to other sites in western China to be "closer to their homes" in the hope that this will __7__ the situation.

Inside the facility, workers were busily stringing nets between dormitory buildings to try to catch any further jumpers. "It is a __8__ solution, but it may save lives," said Mr Gou. The company, which also makes dozens of electronic goods for the likes of Dell, Sony and HP, is also now blocking windows and locking doors to roofs and balconies.

An undercover team of seven Chinese investigators infiltrated the Longhua plant one week ago and told The Daily Telegraph that the __9__ for the mass suicides is "inside the factory" rather than any personal or social __10__ .

Discussion

Discuss the following questions with your class.

1. Do you think Foxconn is a sweatshop?

2. Why do you think so many Foxconn workers commit suicides?

3. What can we do to improve Chinese workers' living conditions?

4. What problems in Chinese economy are exposed through Foxconn suicides?

Section B

Social Media at Work—Bane or Boon?

By Anthony Balderrama

March 9, 2010

(**CareerBuilder. com**)—Social media are, by definition, supposed to be a social experience. Make a profile and start connecting. Reach out to friends, old and new. Post a profile picture, and while you're at it upload a photo album of your trip to Greece so others can see and comment.

When you're done with that, look at your friends' profiles and see what they're up to. Oh, a friend just logged in, too, so now you can chat.

What, it's been two hours since you logged on? How did the time pass so quickly? You should get back to work.

And this is why some employers have banned social media sites—as well as other potential time wasters—from the office. The only problem is that social media aren't a fad. Certain sites might have come and gone over the past five years, but the movement toward interactive communities continues, and companies are active participants.

In fact, having social media skills on your résumé is a boon right now, when many of today's employers haven't ever logged on to Facebook or Twitter and don't understand what these sites do.

The case against social media

Few employers would argue that social networks are inherently bad, but what makes the sites great (freedom to post what's on your mind, discuss the day's hot topics, post silly pictures) is also what makes the sites dangerous for a company. Consider these findings from a 2009 survey on policies and data loss risks from Proofpoint Inc. :

· 17 percent of companies report that they have investigated the posting of confidential, sensitive or private information to a social network, such as Facebook or LinkedIn.

· 10 percent have taken disciplinary actions against an employee who violated social networking policies in the past 12 months.

· 8 percent terminated an employee for violating a social networking policy.

· 45 percent are highly concerned about unauthorized information being posted on social networks.

Even the most ardent Facebooker can see that employers have reason to be concerned about security breaches. Factor in the issue of wasting time and you have a viable threat to productivity. Or is it all sound and fury?

Dona Hall works in a commercial real-estate firm where Facebook and MySpace are banned from any computer connected to the network. Sites for shopping and watching sports are also restricted. Yet, Hall points out that employees could use a smart phone to connect to any of these sites and the company couldn't stop them. She says she thinks that doing so wouldn't address the problem, however.

"As a manager, the focus needs to be on tasked results and productivity, not merely taking the toys away and hoping they don't find something else with which to play," Hall says.

Site forbidden

Nan York works for a corporation that has blocked several Web sites, including Facebook, and her work experience is worse as a result.

"I am not more productive for it. I worked hard for my employer before the ban, and appreciated having something I really enjoyed doing in my few minutes of break from my work," York says. "I am a grown-up and take my grown-up responsibilities very seriously—from paying my bills to doing my work. I don't need stodgy, out-of-touch corporate drones to censure me."

For York, the situation is an issue of trust, or lack thereof, by her bosses.

"They don't trust their work force to differentiate between appropriate and inappropriate media in the workplace, or to do work when on the job," she says.

Book Masters Distribution has found one solution, says marketing coordinator Kim Swanstrom. The company has blocked all social networking sites, as well as streaming media and other potentially objectionable or harmful pages.

"As I do understand the importance, it does become extremely annoying when I am researching things and am constantly being blocked," Swanstrom says. "We try to keep up with what is being said about our books and our company on social networking sites. Our solution has been to set up a community computer in plain sight that has no restrictions."

Other organizations, such as the Patrick Hoover Law Offices, use social media for their businesses. At Hoover Law, employees and interns are encouraged to access and utilize social media as they see fit because it can help the business. Facebook has been successful in getting new clients and publicity for the firm. Plus, the organization can tout its tech-savvy approach to business, not to mention the effect that access to social media has on employee morale.

Obviously, companies haven't formed a uniform stance on social media, and based on their varying experiences, a single approach might not be the best way to handle it. If Facebook can benefit your company, why would you ban it? If employees are wasting time and bandwidth, does it make sense to allow it?

Ultimately employees' best chance of avoiding this battle is to keep the social networking to a minimum while on the clock. Don't give the boss a reason to dislike social media and you won't have to resort to crouching under your desk to check Facebook on your iPhone.

http://edition. cnn. com/2010/LIVING/worklife/03/08/cb. social. media.

banned/index. html

Vocabulary

Match each word to its definition

1. bane   (   )   a. a representation of something in outline

2. boon   (   )   b. a source of harm or ruin

3. profile   (   )   c. a timely benefit

4. upload   (   )   d. existing in possibility

5. potential   (   )   e. mutually or reciprocally active

6. interactive (   )   f. to transfer (as data or files) from a computer to the memory of another device

7. block   (   )   g. a limitation on the use or enjoyment of property or a facility

8. stream   (   )   h. to make unsuitable for passage or progress by obstruction

9. restriction (   )   i. to emit freely or in a stream

10. client   (   )   j. a person who engages the professional advice or services of another

Discussion

Discuss the following questions with your class.

1. Do you support social media sites are banned in companies?

2. What do you think of Chinese government blocking Facebook or Twitter sites in Mainland?

3. Have you often logged on to renren or microblog? Have you enjoyed yourself from them?

4. How should companies motivate their employees to create more productivity?

■ **Section C** ■

Do Open Marriages Work?

By Karen Salmansohn

March 23, 2010

(OPRAH.com)—Can we talk? I mean really talk? I was deeply involved with a man (let's call him Steve) when he surprised me with an unusual request. One night, Steve explained that if and when we got married, he would always want to have a separate apartment where he could be "alone."

In his version of our lives, Steve's "alone" was when he would step out on our relationship—up to three nights a week. Steve wanted an open marriage—a nonmonogamous, polyamorous arrangement wherein he could go his way and I could go mine.

Steve made his request after he and I were intimately involved—catching me totally off guard. I'm a nice Jewish girl from Philadelphia who grew up in a cul de sac where we played kickball and said "darn" instead of "damn" when we missed a kick. The concept of open marriage is very foreign to me, but I do consider myself open-minded. I was already in love with Steve, so wondered, "Was four-sevenths of a marriage to Steve better than no marriage at all?"

Was it at all possible that the pros of an open marriage agreement could outweigh its cons? We all know that deceiving someone you love feels horrible on both sides—so could creating a system of rules for cheating actually prove to be helpful? Does operating with transparency when cheating lessen the stress of an affair? Is the true immorality of cheating the act of dishonesty rather than the act of sex itself?

Here's what I learned about open marriages—the good, the bad and the @ # $ @ !

The Good

When open marriages work, it is most likely because the unconventional unions are focused on good old-fashioned open communication. Telling the truth shows your partner respect, as does following agreed upon rules—for example, keeping your partner in the loop as to where you have been and who you have been with.

The goal of an open marriage is to never have to lie—to create an environment where you can be open about anything that makes you uncomfortable or afraid. Proponents say that this atmosphere supposedly then creates an opportunity for incredible communication, deeper intimacy and the opportunity to thrive as your fullest self.

Basically, the thought is that if you truly love your partner, you want them to live their fullest life—flings and all. Flings are simply superficial sensory delights. There's no difference between your partner enjoying a pizza with anchovies without you and your partner enjoying a blonde with blue eyes without you.

In a good open marriage, you are simply creating a buffet of sexual experiences, so nobody feels like they are starving for new sensations. This honesty enables couples to avoid the emotional downward spiral of hidden affairs because the need for secrecy is removed.

And what about that green-eyed monster jealousy? Most open marriages make strong distinctions between sex with others and romance with others. Couples who subscribe to open-marriage philosophies typically agree to keep their spouses first at heart—no matter who else they mingle with.

The Bad

I must confess, every time I type the words "good open marriage," my fingers twitch. These words feel oxymoronic. Personally, I view more cons than pros to an open marriage. For me, the whole point of marriage is to show your love and commitment by protecting your union with fidelity. There's a great deal of calm and security that comes from knowing your partner is directing his love and attention to you and you alone.

For me, rather than viewing open marriage as offering a yummy buffet of taste sensations, I view it as one big recipe for disaster. The main ingredients—resentment, competitiveness, jealousy, insecurity, curtailed time, scattered affections, feelings of betrayal, lack of security—all inevitably blur the lines of a healthy marriage.

For me, a healthy marriage asks you both to bring out your highest selves. Sure, it might take a little higher willpower to resist the lure of extracurricular sex, but this discipline is for the higher good, allowing for a calm, secure refuge to emerge. Calm and security may not sound as hotsy totsy as sex and more sex, but many of us believe it brings far more happiness in the long run. This security brings with it the confidence of knowing your partner is committed to you "till death do you part" rather than until their next Wednesday evening date.

In my opinion, open marriage is pretty much the opposite of marriage. It seems to be about avoiding commitment—one of the cornerstones of a happy marriage. You may be able to agree on the "rules for cheating" in an intellectual way, but doesn't the emotional nature of love always get in the way?

The "# $ @ %^!"

By the end of my research, I firmly believed that open marriage is merely an excuse for getting away with behaving self-indulgently and recklessly. In my book "Prince Harming Syndrome", any man who wants an open marriage is what I call a Prince Harming. Prince Harming is someone who does not make his partner feel safe, calm, secure, confident—and the idea of an open marriage does not leave me feeling that way.

Dating is for making the most of your options. Marriage is for nurturing the one wonderful union you've been lucky enough to find so it grows into something incredibly wonderful.

It was surprisingly difficult to find statistics on whether open marriages work. Ironically, open marriage isn't something we talk about all that openly. Some research suggests that open marriage has a 92 percent failure rate. Steve Brody, Ph. D. , a psychologist in Cambria, California, explains that less than 1 percent of married people are in open marriages. Nevertheless, it does seem to be a trend on the upturn. Several online dating sites offer applicants a new box to check— married.

So what happened to Steve? I said no to his suggestion for an apartment he'd go to three days a week. You can't be four-sevenths married. If you are going to cheat, why bother asking someone to marry you in the first place?

http://edition. cnn. com/2010/LIVING/personal/03/23/o. open. marriages. work/index. html

Discussion

Discuss the following questions with your class.

1. Can you accept open marriages?

2. What do you think of Swingers' case?

3. Do you believe "seven-year itch" in marriages?

4. What does marriage mean to you?

Unit Eight

Politics

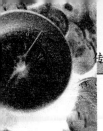

Section A

New Japanese Prime Minister Naoto Kan
Promises to Rebuild Country

The Issue in the News

Naoto Kan was a patent lawyer, who entered politics from a background in left-wing social activism. He is an admirer of Tony Blair, and came to national prominence in 1996.

Mr. Kan is the fifth prime minister in less than five years, and he faces a range of immediate problems from controlling Japan's rising levels of government debt to steering his floundering party through an election next month for seats in Japan's upper house. He won 291 of 420 votes in the DPJ poll defeating his rival, the little known Shinji Tarutoko. Such is the DPJ's majority in the Japanese Diet, that nothing could then stop him from being elected this afternoon as the country's 61st prime minister.

He is expected to keep to the broad policies outlined by Mr Hatoyama, when he won a landslide victory in last summer's general election. His task will be to improve on his predecessor's weak leadership which angered and alienated his own party, Japan's ally, the United States, and the voters who elected him.

He is known to favour a weaker yen, and a rise in Japan's 5 percent consumption tax to reduce government debt and fund the party's ambitious welfare programmes. He also promised to pursue the goal of cutting greenhouse gas emissions by 25 percent by 2020 from 1990 levels.

Points to Notice

As you may read, pay attention to the following facets and information mentioned in this piece of news:

- Naoto Kan's promise to rebuild the nation
- Problems Naoto Kan is confronted with
- Naoto Kan's foreign policy toward US
- Naoto Kan's focus on economy
- Supportive rate for the Democrats

Text

By Justin McCurry

4 June 2010

Fifth leader in four years voted in by ruling Democrats after Yukio Hatoyama's resignation over economy and US airbase.

The Japanese finance minister who started his political career as a straight-talking former civic activist today became the country's fifth prime minister in less than four years.

Naoto Kan[1] beat his only rival, the relatively unknown Shinji Tarutoko, in a vote among MPs of the ruling Democratic party. He immediately promised to "rebuild the country" as it confronts economic stagnation, mounting public debt and regional instability.

The leadership election was called after the resignation on Wednesday of Yukio Hatoyama[2], following his humiliating climbdown over the location of a US airbase and his failure to stamp out sleaze in his own party.

Kan, 63, vowed to rebuild Japan's battered public finances, foster growth and promote regional stability amid growing fears about Chinese military power and tensions on the Korean peninsula.

"My task is to rebuild this nation," said Kan, who was later confirmed as prime minister in the Democrat-dominated lower house. Media reports said he would wait until early next week before naming a cabinet.

With key upper house elections only weeks away, Kan implored party members to re-engage with the voters who had elected them by a landslide last August, ending more than 50 years of almost uninterrupted rule by the conservative Liberal Democratic party.

"We will work together as one in the face of the tough political situation... and fight as a united force," he said.

Kan offered placatory words to the US, whose intransigence over the relocation of Futenma airbase was a major factor in his predecessor's downfall.

During last year's election campaign, Hatoyama had promised to move the marine corps' Futenma base off Okinawa but, under pressure from the White House, was forced to accept an original agreement to move it from its city centre location to a more remote site on the island's north coast.

Kan described relations with the US as "vital", but said he would forge ahead with plans to create an east Asian community modelled on the EU. "While the US-Japan alliance is the cornerstone of our diplomacy, we must also work for the prosperity of the Asian region," he said.

He repeated Hatoyama's pledge to cut Japan's greenhouse gas emissions by

25% over the next 10 years from 1990 levels.

Analysts said Kan's immediate focus should be Japan's stuttering economy. An export-led recovery is under way thanks to demand in China, but Japan is battling deflation and unemployment, and a public debt that, according to some estimates, is around 200% of GDP.

As Hatoyama's finance minister, Kan favoured a weaker yen and pressured Japan's central bank to take a more active role in fighting deflation. Unlike his predecessor, he has not ruled out what would doubtlessly be an unpopular rise in the consumption [sales] tax to meet ballooning health and welfare costs.

"Kan taking office will be good for a weaker yen but he is considering raising the consumption tax, which will have a negative impact on the stock market," said Yoshikiyo Shimamine, chief economist at the Dai-ichi Life Research Institute in Tokyo.

"If he fully advocates fiscal reform over a growth strategy, it would be difficult for the government to secure funds for some of the party's policies, such as allowances for families with children."

The political turmoil of the last few days has heightened investor anxiety over whether the new government will delay its plans, due out later this month, to rein in public debt and encourage growth.

After Hatoyama's resignation, just eight months after taking office, the Democrats are hoping that Kan's arrival will herald a period of stability and boost their flagging fortunes five weeks before upper house elections.

Although the party has a large majority in the more powerful lower house, significant losses next month will force it to court smaller parties if it wants to maintain a majority in the second chamber and push through key legislation.

New poll figures suggested the departure of Hatoyama, and his scandal-tainted general secretary, Ichiro Ozawa, had already lifted the party's fortunes.

A poll conducted on Wednesday by the Yomiuri Shimbun newspaper found that support for the Democrats had increased to 29%, up 9 points from last weekend, but still well down on the 70% they enjoyed last September.

http://www.guardian.co.uk/world/2010/jun/04/japan-prime-minister-naoto-kan

Vocabulary

1.	resignation	*n.*	when you officially announce that you have decided to leave your job or an organization, or a written statement that says you will be leaving
2.	confront	*vt.*	to deal with something very difficult or unpleasant in a brave and determined way
3.	stagnation	*n.*	not changing or making progress, and continuing to be in a bad condition
4.	humiliating	*adj.*	making you feel ashamed, embarrassed, and angry because you have been made to look weak or stupid
5.	sleaze	*n.*	immoral behavior, especially involving sex or lies
6.	battered	*adj.*	old and in bad condition
7.	confirm	*vt/vi.*	to show that something is definitely true, especially by providing more proof
8.	implore	*vt.*	beg; to ask for something in an emotional way
9.	placatory	*adj.*	to soothe or mollify especially by concessions; to make someone stop feeling angry
10.	intransigence	*n.*	unwilling to change your ideas or behavior, in a way that seems unreasonable
11.	predecessor	*n.*	someone who had your job before you started doing it
12.	alliance	*n.*	an arrangement in which two or more countries, groups etc agree to work together to try to change or achieve something
13.	prosperity	*n.*	the condition of being successful or thriving; especially: economic well-being
14.	emission	*n.*	a gas or other substance that is sent into the air
15.	advocate	*vi.*	to publicly say that something should be done

Language Notes

1. **Naoto Kan**: Prime Minister of Japan. In June 2010, as Finance Minister, Kan was elected as the leader of the Democratic Party of Japan (DPJ) and was designated Prime Minister by the Diet and later by Emperor of Japan, in each instance to succeed Yukio Hatoyama.

2. **Yukio Hatoyama** (鸠山由纪夫 born 11 February 1947): a Japanese politician who became the Prime Minister of Japan on 16 September 2009. On 3 June 2010, Hatoyama resigned as prime minister

Exercises

 Vocabulary and Expressions

A. Idioms and Expressions

Fill in the blanks with the correct idiom or expression.

1. stamp out: prevent something bad from continuing 消除、杜绝

We aim to stamp out poverty in our lifetimes.

2. forge ahead: to make progress and become more and more successful 稳步前进、越来越成功

An increasing number of people have forged ahead in this competitive field.

3. ruled out: to make it impossible for something to happen 使某事不可能发生

The mountainous terrain rules out most forms of agriculture.

1. His hesitation _____ the likelihood of success.

2. The company finally made a decision to _____ the bribes.

3. After the economic depression, the world has _____ in its way.

B. Vocabulary

Fill in the blanks with the words given below. Change the form where necessary.

> confirm sleaze stagnation battered implore
>
> advocate alliance humiliating emission prosperity

1. Although he experienced a _____ defeat, he sticks to his primary decision.

2. Many people are tired of all the _____ on TV.

3. He doesn't want to throw his _____ old suitcase away.

4. Britain agreed to cut _____ of nitrogen oxide from power stations.

5. The government planed to revive the economic _____.

6. New evidence has _____ the first witness's story.

7. In the earthquake-stricken area numerous victims _____ the soldiers to save their loved ones.

8. Britain formed a military _____ with her NATO partners.

9. In the past two decades our nation went through a time of economic _____ _____.

10. Extremists were openly _____ violence.

Exploring Content

A. Complete the sentences based on the reading text.

1. Fifth leader in four years voted in by _____

   _____.

2. Naoto Kan immediately promised to "rebuild the country" as _____

   _____.

3. With key upper house elections only weeks away, Kan implored party members to re-engage with the voters who had elected them by a landslide last August, _____.

4. Naoto Kan said that they will work together as one _____.

5. As Hatoyama's finance minister, Kan favored a weaker yen and _____

   _____.

B. Put a check(✓) next to the statements that the writer would agree with.

1. (　　) The Japanese finance minister who started his political career as a straight-talking former civic activist today became the country's fifth prime minister in less than four years.

2. (　　) The leadership election was called after the resignation on Wednesday of Yukio Hatoyama, following his climb up over the location of a US airbase and his success of stamping out sleaze in his own party.

3. (　　) Kan vowed to rebuild Japan's battered public finances, foster growth and promote regional stability amid growing fears about Chinese military power and tensions on the Korean peninsula.

4. (　　) Kan described relations with the US as "vital", and said he would forge ahead with plans to create an Asian community modeled on the EU.

5. (　　) Kan repeated Hatoyama's pledge to cut Japan's greenhouse gas emissions by 25% over the next 20 years from 1990 levels.

6. (　　) A poll conducted on Wednesday by the Yomiuri Shimbun newspaper found that support for the Democrats had decreased to 29%, still well down on the 70% they enjoyed last September.

 Translation

Translate the following sentences into Chinese.

1. He immediately promised to "rebuild the country" as it confronts economic stagnation, mounting public debt and regional instability.

2. With key upper house elections only weeks away, Kan implored party members to re-engage with the voters who had elected them by a landslide last August.

3. While the US-Japan alliance is the cornerstone of our diplomacy, we must also work for the prosperity of the Asian region.

4. He repeated Hatoyama's pledge to cut Japan's greenhouse gas emissions by 25% over the next 10 years from 1990 levels.

5. Kan taking office will be good for a weaker yen but he is considering raising the consumption tax, which will have a negative impact on the stock market.

✉ Cloze

Complete the following short passage by choosing proper words from the word bank provided.

sworn	latter	address	varying	stagnation	arranged	succeed
revitalise	ranging	former	vigor	appointed	continuity	
enthusiastic	inexperienced					

Japan's new Prime Minister Naoto Kan unveiled his cabinet Tuesday, seeking to __1__ his party's centre-left rule and tackle challenges __2__ from a stagnant economy to strained US relations.

Kan, Japan's fifth premier in four years, announced his cabinet line-up before he was to __3__ the nation in a press conference and then head to the palace of Emperor Akihito to be formally __4__ in.

In a show of __5__ from the previous administration, Kan kept 11 of 17 ministers in their posts, including Foreign Minister Katsuya Okada, Defence Minister Toshimi Kitazawa and Transport Minister Seiji Maehara.

Kan, the __6__ finance minister, chose his deputy, fiscal hawk Yoshihiko Noda, to __7__ him as the steward of Asia's biggest economy.

Noda takes over the job as pressure mounts to revive the economy after two decades of __8__ and to slash Japan's public debt mountain, which is nearly twice the size of the country's gross domestic product.

Reading out the cabinet names was Yoshito Sengoku, who became Kan's right-hand man and press spokesman as chief cabinet secretary.

"Prime Minister Kan has __9__ the ministers mindful of the need to form a government with professionalism, very clean politics and ability to govern," he said, calling the cabinet "young, fresh and __10__ about their jobs."

Kan, a one-time leftist activist popular for his plain-speaking style, is riding an early wave of support, with approval rates above 60 percent, after pledging to clean house in his Democratic Party of Japan (DPJ).

Discussion

Discuss the following questions with your class.

1. What challenges is Naoto Kan facing in Japanese economy when he takes office?

2. What are Naoto Kan's foreign policies?

3. What impact do you think Naoto Kan's decision to raise consumption tax will make on Japanese economy?

4. What did Naoto Kan want to convey by saying he would not visit Yasukuni Shrine during his tenure?

███ **Section B** ███

Health Reform's Winners and Losers

By Brian Wingfield, David Whelan and Matt Herper

March 21 2010

The historic House vote will mean big changes for small businesses, HMOs and many workers.

WASHINGTON—The biggest health care overhaul in nearly half a century is about to become reality.

The House of Representatives passed health care reform legislation Sunday night by a vote of 219-212, effectively ending a year's worth of political horse trading and lobbying. The bill now goes to President Barack Obama for his certain approval. After the vote, House Democrats broke out into a chorus of "Yes we can, yes we can," the signature slogan of Obama's presidential campaign. But the real workings of reform are only now beginning as industry stakeholders, the public and the courts prepare to deal with the fine print of how the legislation will be implemented.

The overhaul gives an additional 32 million Americans access to basic health insurance by 2019, according to the Congressional Budget Office. The biggest change in the American health system since Medicare was enacted in 1965, the reforms are expected to cost $ 938 billion during the next decade. It is going to be paid for by cuts in Medicare, new taxes on investment income and fees on various industry participants—which certainly will be passed along to the general public. But while government subsidies for people who cannot afford insurance and insurance exchanges to help people get insurance won't be operational before 2014, the increased costs will begin next year.

Big changes are coming for small business. Companies with more than 200 workers will be required to automatically enroll their employees in whatever insurance plan they offer. Companies with at least 50 workers are subject to fines if their workers end up receiving government subsidized coverage. The bill also contains tax breaks for small firms that provide employees with health insurance.

The legislation may be going to Obama for signing, but the action isn't over in Congress. Following the passage of the bill, the House passed a so-called " reconciliation bill " to make adjustments to the Senate-defined package. However, the Senate has yet to take up the reconciliation bill. Senate Democrats have assured their counterparts in the House that they have enough votes to pass the reconciliation bill next week. It will only need a simple majority vote. The president would then sign the alterations into law. Assuming the reconciliation process is completed, here's a look at which groups are the biggest winners and losers in health reform:

The Uninsured

According to the Congressional Budget Office, 94% of all non-elderly Americans will have access to health insurance by 2016, vs. 83% now. Health insurers won't be able to deny coverage based on pre-existing conditions. People who elect not to get insurance will have to pay a penalty of $ 695 per year or 2.5% of income (phased in before 2016). But state-based exchanges will be set up to make shopping for an insurance plan easier. Generous subsidies will be available to families that make up to $ 88,000 in household income.

Private Insurers

America's Health Insurance Plans, an industry group for private insurers, has complained that health care reform leaves 23 million Americans uninsured, imposes drastic cuts in Medicare Advantage and levies a $ 70 billion tax hike

(over 10 years) on the industry. While HMOs whine a lot, they actually came out OK. Their biggest nightmare was long ago removed from the legislation: a government-run plan to compete with private companies. Better yet, health insurers get 32 million new taxpayer-subsidized customers. In essence, it's a big Cash for Clunkers program for HMOs.

Among the HMOs, the biggest winners are Cigna (CI-news-people), Aetna (AET-news-people) and United Healthcare because they are concentrated in big employer markets that will be largely unaffected by the bill. The bill is more likely to have a negative impact on WellPoint (WLP-news-people) and Humana (HUM-news-people). WellPoint could lose shelf space in the individual market it now dominates in many states. Humana has a big Medicare Advantage business and will get hammered by the reimbursement cuts.

Drug and Biotech Companies

Drug companies like Merck (MRK-news-people), Pfizer (PFE-news-people) and Amgen (AMGN-news-people) are among the biggest industry winners in the legislation. They suddenly will have tens of millions more insured customers who can afford their expensive medicines. The pharmaceutical industry's trade group was a big supporter of the legislation, and any threats to the industry were stripped out early or never included. There's no real plan for comparing treatments to one another, one approach that could lower costs, or for giving the government power to bargain for lower prices. The bill also gives drug makers extra layers of monopoly protection for protein-based biotech drugs, one of the industry's hottest areas

http://www. forbes. com/2010/03/21/health-care-vote-business-beltway-congress. html? boxes = Homepagetopnew

Vocabulary

Match each word to its definition.

1. overhaul   (   )   a. a law or set of laws

2. legislation   (   )   b. the act of giving someone something and receiving

something else from them

3. campaign　　（　） c. to take action or make changes that you have officially decided should happen

4. insurance　　（　） d. a series of actions intended to achieve a particular result relating to politics or business, or a social improvement

5. implement　　（　） e. if a government or organization subsidizes a company, activity etc, it pays part of its costs

6. subsidized　　（　） f. an arrangement with a company in which you pay them money, especially regularly, and they pay the costs if something bad happens

7. exchange　　（　） g. necessary changes or repairs made to a machine or system

8. reconciliation　（　） h. to hit something with a hammer in order to force it into a particular position or shape

9. monopoly　　（　） i. a situation in which two people, countries etc become friendly with each other again after quarrelling

10. hammered　　（　） j. if a company or government has a monopoly of a business or political activity, it has complete control of it so that other organizations cannot compete with it

Discussion

Discuss the following questions with your class.

1. What's the main content of health care reform bill?

2. Who are the biggest beneficiaries of health care reform?

3. Do you think health care reform can reduce medical costs effectively?

4. Do you think health care reform is weal or woe for the Democratic Party?

Section C

Britain's Election Ends in Political Standoff

May 7, 2010

Associated Press

LONDON—The Conservatives and Labour jockeyed for the support of Britain's smaller parties Friday after a close-fought election that, for the first time in almost four decades, produced no outright winner and left jittery financial markets clamoring for a quick resolution.

As the Conservative Party, which won the largest number of seats, demanded the chance to govern, Liberal Democrat leader Nick Clegg dented Labour Prime Minister Gordon Brown's hopes of staying in power by calling on the Tories to try to form a government, without indicating whether his centrist party would be willing to join a coalition.

But obstacles remained in the way of the Tories. As sitting prime minister, Brown would traditionally be given the first chance to put together a government. His left-of-center Labour Party is seen as a more natural coalition fit with the Liberal Democrats, the third-place party now thrust into the role of potential kingmaker.

But Clegg said the party that had gained the most seats and the most votes—the Conservatives—should have "the first right to seek to govern."

"I think it is now for the Conservative Party to prove that it is capable of seeking to govern in the national interest," he said.

Despite winning the largest number of House of Commons seats in Thursday's election, David Cameron's Conservatives fell short of a majority that only a few months ago was considered inevitable. Labour was on track to lose nearly 90 seats in Parliament but still could govern with the help of the Liberal Democrats. Clegg's party surprisingly failed to capitalize on his stellar TV debate performances, but still could hold the keys to Downing St. for one of the other parties. His support is sure to be contingent on a promise of electoral reform, the Lib Dems' main demand.

That may be an insuperable sticking point for the Conservatives. Many of the party's old guard distrust the Liberal Democrats' pro-European leanings and fiercely oppose its call for proportional representation, which would make it hard for any single party to hold power alone—effectively shutting out the Conservatives indefinitely.

"The Tories would fight it (electoral reform) tooth and nail," said Bill Jones, professor of politics at Liverpool Hope University. "It's like asking a turkey to vote for Christmas."

Labour is much more amenable to demands for electoral reform, but even a deal with the Liberal Democrats would leave them a few seats short of a majority, meaning they would have to turn to Scottish and Welsh nationalists for further support.

Scottish national party leader Alex Salmond, whose party won six seats, said he had already been invited to talks with Brown.

"Fate seems to have dealt us a mighty hand between ourselves and (Welsh nationalists) Plaid Cymru," Salmond told the BBC.

With 633 of the 650 seats counted, the Conservatives had secured 299 seats, Labour 253, the Liberal Democrats 54 and smaller parties, 27 seats. At least 326 of the House of Commons' 650 seats are needed to form a government with a majority.

"The country has spoken—but we don't know what they've said," former

Liberal Democrat leader Paddy Ashdown said, summing up confusion.

Days, and possibly weeks, of political horse-trading could lie ahead—a prospect that gave the financial markets jitters.

As the pound and the FTSE-100 index fell sharply, pressure mounted for a quick solution.

"A decision would have to be made very quickly," said Victoria Honeyman, a lecturer in politics at the University of Leeds,

She predicted that some sort of statement would have to be made before Monday when the markets reopen.

"There's a limit to how long can that this go on," she said. "The pound will start to crash."

Talks were expected to begin between political players Friday, aided by civil service guidelines detailing how the process should unfold.

Although Britain has no written constitution, senior civil servants have been preparing furiously to lay out the rules and avoid market-rattling uncertainty in the event of a so-called hung parliament, a result in which no party secures a majority. The last time a British election produced such a result was in 1974.

A period of political wrangling and confusion in one of the world's largest economies could unsettle global markets already reeling from the Greek debt crisis and fears of wider debt contagion in Europe. Britain's budget deficit is set to eclipse even that of Greece next year, and whoever winds up in power faces the daunting challenge of introducing big government spending cuts to slash the country's huge deficit.

In London, bond trading started in the middle of the night—six hours earlier than normal—as traders tried to make sense of the election results. Britain's main stock index and the pound fell Friday as investors reacted to the inconclusive result against a backdrop of global market turbulence.

In the first minute of trading, the FTSE 100 share index was down 1.3 percent at 5,193 before rallying slightly above 5,200. The British pound traded as low as $ 1.46589 by early afternoon, down from $ 1.51 less than 24 hours earlier.

The Conservatives insisted they had been given a mandate by the electorate. Cameron said voters had rejected Brown and his Labour Party.

"Our country wants change. That change is going to require new leadership," Cameron said Friday.

Cameron planned to make a statement at 2:30 p. m. (1330 GMT, 9:30 a. m. EDT), which his party said would outline his plan for "strong and stable" government.

Brown also vowed to "play my part in Britain having a strong, stable" government and indicated he would seek an alliance with the Liberal Democrats, pledging action on election reform—a key demand of his would-be partners.

Turnout for the election—the closest-fought in a generation—was 65. 2 percent, higher than the 61 percent seen in Britain's 2005 election.

Some polling stations around the country were overwhelmed by those interested in casting ballots, and hundreds of people were blocked from voting due to problems with Britain's old-fashioned paper ballot system.

Anger flared when voters in London, Sheffield, Newcastle and elsewhere complained that they had been blocked from voting as stations closed—and the head of Britain's Electoral Commission said some legal challenges to results because of blocked votes were likely.

Electoral Commission chief Jenny Watson acknowledged that Britain's paper voting system had been unable to cope with a surge of voters.

Former British Home Secretary Jacqui Smith was the biggest Labour lawmaker to lose her seat after being caught attempting to bill the public for porn movies watched by her husband.

But Labour won the northern England seat of Rochdale—where Brown made the biggest gaffe of the campaign, caught on an open microphone referring to an elderly voter as a "bigoted woman" after she buttonholed him on immigration. Brown later visited her home to apologize.

In the southern England resort town of Brighton, Britain's first-ever Green

Party lawmaker, Caroline Lucas, was elected.

The Conservatives were ousted by Labour under Tony Blair in 1997 after 18 years in power. Three leaders and three successive election defeats later, the party selected Cameron, a fresh-faced, bicycle-riding graduate of Eton and Oxford who promised to modernize its fusty, right-wing image.

Under Brown, who took over from Blair three years ago, Britain's once high-flying economy, rooted in world-leading financial services, has run into hard times. In addition, at least 1.3 million people have been laid off and tens of thousands have lost their homes in a crushing recession.

http://www.foxnews.com/world/2010/05/06/britons-vote-close-election/

Discussion

Discuss the following questions with your class.

1. Faced with cutting financial deficits and reinvigorating economy, how do the Conservative and the Liberal Democrats keep balance?

2. What problems does the coalition government bring out in British parliamentary system?

3. How can you explain the phenomenon that Gordon Brown worked very successfully as the Chancellor of the Exchequer but failed to be a successful prime minister?

4. What is the administrative programme of coalition government?

Unit **N**ine

Travel

Section A

A Quick Stop in Old Cuba

Dancers in front of a facade of an Old Havana storefront at last year's
Cuba Nostalgia Fair in Miami.

The Issue in the News

Cuba Nostalgia is a three-day celebration of all things Cuban, held one weekend each May at Miami's Fair Expo Center. It's like taking a trip back to Havana's glory days. Cuba Nostalgia features live Cuban music, traditional Cuban foods, performers, and vendors. To get a more authentic Cuban experience, you'd have to travel all the way back to Havana! The annual Cuba Nostalgia event is one great big party with everyone welcome, Cubans, and non-Cubans alike. Vendors from all over Miami and elsewhere are on hand to sell jewelry, photographs, coins, maps, music, books, and other memorabilia. There are plenty of beautiful examples of a bygone era, when everything in Havana had a distinct style and grace. Cuba Nostalgia also showcases the works of many Cuban artists with most artwork available for sale. For many people who escaped Castro's Cuba, this may be the last chance to relive some old memories.

Points to Notice

As you read, pay attention to the following facets and information mentioned in this piece of news:

- Havana
- Miami
- Cuba Nostalgia fair
- Pre-Castro era
- Wilfredo Lam—the Picasso of Cuba

Text

By Brett Sokol

May 16, 2010

FOR most Americans, Havana[1] remains—as a Cuban tourism official recently quipped to a reporter—"the forbidden city," subject to a United States travel ban and enticingly off-limits. A steady trickle of American visitors continues to slip into the city via flights from Cancún and Nassau, quietly testing the Obama administration's de facto "don't ask, don't tell" Cuban travel policy at overseas customs desks. But why risk a steep fine when you can instead wing on down to Miami[2] for next weekend's 12th annual Cuba Nostalgia fair at the Miami-Dade County Fair Expo Center? Organizers expect a crowd of 30,000 for three days of Cuban art, music, food and, not least, shopping.

Just don't go looking to buy a Che Guevara T-shirt. The focus of Cuba Nostalgia, as its name implies, is exclusively on the country's pre-Castro era: Its promoters promise "a journey back in time for those who remember the island's glamorous times—and for those who never experienced them."

"For every year you live in Miami you hear 20,000 stories about Cuba," said Leslie Pantín Jr., a local advertising executive and a founder of the fair who fled the island with his family as an 11-year-old in 1960. Fifty years later, "you get confused," he admitted. "Sometimes when I'm talking about Havana, I can't remember if it's my own memory, if somebody told me about it, or if I looked it up in a book of photos." Indeed, the fair's gathering of the Cuban-exile community can take on a bittersweet air, evoking both celebration and loss.

As in previous years, elderly couples will be able to linger over a giant aerial photo of 1953 Havana, pointing out their former homes (some abandoned, others seized) to their children and grandchildren. A mock-up of the swanky El Encanto department store will elicit shouts of recognition from those who recall life before the 1959 revolution. And a replica of the iconic Malecón, the sea wall that runs around Havana's waterfront, will draw even recent arrivals from Cuba to pose for snapshots.

Sprawled across the center's 100,000 square feet, the event's cultural exhibits and memorabilia vendors cater to both high-and low-brow tastes: You'll find Surrealist works by Wilfredo Lam, known as the Picasso of Cuba, as well as black-velvet tributes to the island's bygone boxing champions. "Art is a very elastic word within Cuban nostalgia," Mr. Pantín said. "Anything goes, as long as it's not pictures of Fidel or Raúl. Or pornography."

You can also buy vintage issues of Bohemia magazine, the Cuban chattering class's answer to The New Yorker (before it was nationalized and turned into a Communist Party mouthpiece), and perfect facsimiles of the 1958 Havana phonebook (making this corner of Miami the only place in America where a bound copy of the Yellow Pages is still in demand). And Cuban coffee is available at the decidedly '50s-era price point of 3 cents a shot.

Regardless of whatever rapprochement the future holds, Mr. Pantín said Cuba Nostalgia—the fair and the feeling—will endure. "The history we show no longer exists in Cuba, " he said. " How else will younger people learn about this era?"

Cuba Nostalgia runs from May 21 to 23 at the Miami-Dade County Fair Expo Center, 10901 Southwest 24th Street, Miami; (305) 856-7595; cubanostalgia. org. Admission is $ 12 for adults, $ 6 for age 9 and younger.

http://travel. nytimes. com/pages/travel/index. html

Online Resources

http://travel. nytimes. com/travel/guides/europe/turkey/overview. html

http://travel. nytimes. com/2010/06/27/travel/27hours. html? ref = travel

http://frugaltraveler. blogs. nytimes. com/

http://travel. nytimes. com/2010/06/27/travel/27choice. html? ref = travel

Vocabulary

1.	quip	vi.	to say something clever and amusing
2.	enticingly	adv.	in an attractive manner
3.	off-limits	adj.	not to be entered or patronized by a designated class
4.	trickle	n.	a: to issue or fall in drops b: to flow in a thin gentle stream
5.	de facto	adj.	(formal) really existing although not legally stated to exist
6.	flee	vi.	to leave somewhere very quickly, in order to escape from danger
7.	exile	n.	a situation in which you are forced to leave your country and live in another country, especially for political reasons
8.	evoke	vi.	to produce a strong feeling or memory in someone
9.	aerial	adj.	in or moving through the air
10.	mock-up	n.	a full size model of something, made before the real thing is built, or made for a film, show etc
11.	replica	n.	an exact copy of something, especially a building, a gun,

or a work of art

12. memorabilia	n.	things that you keep or collect because they are connected with a famous person, event, or time
13. surrealist	n.	20th century art or literature in which the artist or writer connects unrelated images and objects in a strange way
14. tribute	n.	something that you say, do, or give in order to express your respect or admiration for someone
15. elastic	a.	capable of being easily stretched or expanded and resuming former shape
16. pornography	n.	magazines, films etc that show sexual acts and images in a way that is intended to make people feel sexually excited
17. vintage	adj.	showing all the best or most typical qualities of something
18. facsimile	n.	an exact copy of a picture, piece of writing etc
19. rapprochement	n.	the establishment of a good relationship between two countries or groups of people, after a period of unfriendly relations

Language Notes

1. **Havana**: the capital city, major port, and leading commercial centre of Cuba. The city is one of the 14 Cuban provinces. The city/province has 2. 1 million inhabitants, the largest city in Cuba and the second largest in the Caribbean region. The city extends mostly westward and southward from the bay, which is entered through a narrow inlet and which divides into three main harbours: Marimelena, Guanabacoa, and Atarés.

2. **Miami**: a major city located on the Atlantic coast in southeastern Florida. Miami is the county seat of Miami-Dade County, the most populous county in Florida. It is the principal city and the center of the South Florida metropolitan area, which had a 2008 population of 5,414,712, ranking 7th largest in the U. S.

Exercises

✉ **Vocabulary and Expressions**

A. Idioms and Expressions

Fill in the blanks with the correct idiom or expression.

slip into：go somewhere quietly or quickly 溜进

He slipped into an indigo tank.

take on：to assume or acquire as or as if one's own 接受,承担

We can't take on any more work we're fully stretched（ie working to the utmost of our powers）at the moment.

linger over：be slow 动作迟缓,拖沓,磨蹭

linger over one's meal

1. He is unwilling to _____ heavy responsibilities.

2. She always _____ her work.

3. Mother _____ the room of her child and tucked him up.

B. Vocabulary

Fill in the blanks with the words given below. Change the form where necessary.

quip enticingly off-limits trickle flee exile evoke
aerial replica memorabilia surrealist tribute elastic facsimile

1. That old movie _____ memories of my childhood.

2. Unlike most group discussions, nothing was _____.

3. I'd like to pay the _____ to the party workers for all their hard work.

4. "Giving up smoking is easy," he _____. "I've done it hundreds of times."

5. Masaari spent six months in prison before _____ the country.

6. Rubber is _____.

7. It was a hot day and the water looked _____.

8. Equipment used to produce such a graph or tracing in _____ transmission.

9. The water in the stream had been reduced to a _____.

10. He was in the unenviable position of having to choose between imprisonment or _____.

11. The birds perched on the television _____.

12. I had a _____ in little of Independence Hall.

✉ **Exploring Content**

A. Read the following statements, and then mark T (True) if the statement agrees with the information given in the passage, mark F (False) if the statement contradicts the information given in the passage.

1. _____ A steady trickle of American visitors continues to slip into Havana via flights from Cancún and Nassau.

2. _____ Organizers expect a crowd of 300,000 for three days of Cuban art, music, food and, not least, shopping.

3. _____ As in previous years, elderly couples will be able to linger over a giant aerial photo of 1953 Havana, pointing out their former homes (some abandoned, others seized) to their children and grandchildren.

4. _____ Sprawled across the center's 100,000 square feet, the event's cultural exhibits and memorabilia vendors cater to only high-brow taste.

5. _____ Cuba Nostalgia runs from May 20 to 23 at the Miami-Dade County Fair Expo Center, 10901 Southwest 24th Street, Miami

B. Find the synonym in the reading.

1. Find a word in Paragraph 1 that means *being or characterized by a rapid and intensive decline or increase.* _____

2. Find a word in Paragraph 2 that means *only.* _____

3. Find a word in Paragraph 3 that means *unable to understand or think clearly what someone is saying or what is happening.* _____

4. Find a word in Paragraph 4 that means *to succeed in getting information or a reaction from someone, especially when this is difficult.* _____

5. Find a word in Paragraph 5 that means *a feeling that a time in the past was*

good, or the activity of remembering a good time in the past and wishing that things had not changed. _____

 Translation

Translate the following sentences into Chinese.

1. A steady trickle of American visitors continues to slip into the city via flights from Cancún and Nassau, quietly testing the Obama administration's de facto "don't ask, don't tell" Cuban travel policy at overseas customs desks.

2. Organizers expect a crowd of 30,000 for three days of Cuban art, music, food and, not least, shopping.

3. "Sometimes when I'm talking about Havana, I can't remember if it's my own memory, if somebody told me about it, or if I looked it up in a book of photos."

4. As in previous years, elderly couples will be able to linger over a giant aerial photo of 1953 Havana, pointing out their former homes (some abandoned, others seized) to their children and grandchildren.

5. And Cuban coffee is available at the decidedly '50s-era price point of 3 cents a shot.

 Cloze

Complete the following short passage by choosing proper words from the word bank provided.

back soared ellipse heating collapse available access through
increasing tropical tourism devoted due drop alliance

Cuba hopes to attract some 45,000 Russian tourists this year, officials said Monday, targeting nostalgia for the communist island's long-running __1__ with the former Cold War superpower. Having __2__ 22 percent so far this year over 2009 figures, Tourism Minister Joseph Bieber at the 30th International Tourism Fair __3__ to Russian tourists said the economic crisis had caused a __4__ in visitors last year. Alexander Radkov, vice president of the Russian Federal Tourism Agency, attended the fair highlighting the Caribbean island's wealth of beautiful white sand beaches and

___5___ sun, along with dozens of Russian business representatives. Havana's secret weapon for Russian tourists is nostalgia, officials said, playing off a 30-year relationship between the countries ___6___ to a once strong political and economic alliance between them. Relations deteriorated following the Soviet Union's ___7___ in 1991, but ties have been growing ___8___ over the last five years. ___9___ is Cuba's second largest economic sector after medical services, and it has a total of 47,000 rooms ___10___ in 300 tourist hotels around the island.

Discussion

Discuss the following questions with your class.

1. What do you know of Cuba?

2. Which style of building do you like most? Share it with your friends.

3. Do you know the Picasso of Cuba? Try to search out as much information as you can about it.

4. Have you visited the 2010 Shanghai World Expo? If yes, share your experience with your friends.

■ Section B ■

ZTA Hails A'Sambeni's Pulling Power

THE Zimbabwe Tourism Authority (ZTA) acting chief executive officer, Givemore Chidzidzi has said the A'Sambeni travel expo held in Bulawayo recently has given exhibitors the chance to see that the country's tourism industry has recovered. A'Sambeni is an annual travel expo held concurrently with the Zimbabwe International Trade Fair.

This year's edition of the expo attracted 59 exhibitors from Britain and Italy. Last year there were 39 exhibitors, Chidzidzi said.

"We have shown them (exhibitors) the hospitality in Zimbabwe and they are coming back in October for Sanganai/Hlanganani," he said.

Sanganai/Hlanganani is Zimbabwe's largest travel and tourism trade expo held annually in October and has been slotted on the United Nations World Tourism Organisation calendar.

Chidzidzi said ZTA had embarked on hosting programmes like A'Sambeni and Miss Tourism to spruce up the country's image.

"We are having a perception management programme where we bring in brave people from abroad to visit our country so that they send back messages about Zimbabwe. We want people to think twice about Zimbabwe," Chidzidzi said.

The tourism product is tired and requires attention but operators do not have capital to fund major refurbishments.

Local operators are turning to regional financial institutions for long-term funding which is not available locally.

ZTA hopes that the hosting of the FIFA World Cup in South Africa will send out favourable signals about Zimbabwe's tourism sector.

"Southern Africa will benefit in the long term from the publicity produced by 2010," Chidzidzi said.

"We, as the government are thinking of the long-term challenges we will face in trying to sustain good publicity before and after the World Cup. "

Visiting journalists said there were opportunities for investment in the tourism industry.

Cindy Lou Dale, a British writer and photojournalist said she saw many opportunities for investment in Zimbabwe during the tour.

"Zimbabwe needs to reclaim the brains that have left for other countries," she said.

"There is no need for capital investment from foreign countries. It's time Zimbabwe pushed bureaucracy aside and used the brains that they have. "

Dale called upon Zimbabweans abroad to engage in promoting Zimbabwean tourism while acting as ambassadors for the country.

Zimbabwe's tourism industry is recovering from a decade of a slow down due to the bad publicity owing to an unstable political and economic environment.

http://allafrica. com/stories/201005030983. html

Vocabulary

Match each word to its definition.

1. concurrently   (   )   a. to get back something that you have lost or that has been taken away from you

2. hospitality   (   )   b. the upgrading of a building's fabric and services with the aim of enhancing its ability to compete effectively for tenants, improve rental growth,

and maximise market value.

3. slot ( ) c. existing or happening at the same time

4. embark ( ) d. the attention that someone or something gets from newspapers, television etc:

5. spruce ( ) e. friendly behaviour towards visitors:

6. refurbishment ( ) f. a complicated official system which is annoying or confusing because it has a lot of rules, processes etc

7. publicity ( ) g. to go into a slot, or to put something in a slot

8. reclaim ( ) h. to go onto a ship or a plane, or to put or take something onto a ship or plane

9. bureaucracy ( ) i. (informal) to make yourself or something look neater and tidier Discussion

Discussion

Discuss the following questions with your class.

1. What does this article tell us?

2. Do you like traveling? Will you visit some of the African countries in the future?

3. How much do you know about Zimbabwe?

4. Talk about your favorite traveling places or countries.

■ Section C ■

New Travel Guides, from Lonely Planet to Luxury

By Beth J. Harpaz, Ap Travel Editor

Apr 27,2010

NEW YORK—Spring is the time when many travelers plan their biggest vacations of the year: Leisurely road trips, family getaways with kids out of school, and travel abroad over the peak summer season. Here are some of the new guidebook releases from this season to inspire you and help plan your itineraries. They include titles from Lonely Planet, Frommer's, DK Eyewitness, a luxury hotel group, and Budget Travel.

LONELY PLANET'S DISCOVER SERIES: Once upon a time, the stereotypical Lonely Planet reader was an adventurous young backpacker on a budget, ready to rough it and explore. But today Lonely Planet fans include older travelers, travelers who don't mind spending more for comfort, and travelers looking for advice about basics and must-sees, not just offbeat adventures.

To cater to this audience, Lonely Planet has launched a new series called "Discover," with thick $ 25 paperback books just released on Australia, France, Great Britain, Ireland, Italy, Japan, Spain and Thailand. The books are ideal for planning one-to two-week trips.

"Discover Europe" will be added to the series May 10.

The full-color books include maps, best-of lists, recommendations for a variety of budgets, tips from locals on visiting major attractions, and suggested itineraries organized by region, theme and length of trip. One especially nice touch: "If You Like" features direct readers to less well-known attractions by comparing them to better-known places. For example, the Venice section of the Italy guide says that "If you like the masterpieces of the Peggy Guggenheim Collection, we think you'll like these other modern art gems," and it goes on to list Ca' Pesaro and Museo della Fondazione Querini Stampalia.

FROMMER'S DAY BY DAY GUIDES: Frommer's "Day by Day" city guides have been among the brand's best-selling books for years. Earlier this year, Frommer's launched full-size "Day by Day" guides to countries, states and other large regions. The full-color books are itinerary-based, include more than 100 maps and a pocket with a large pullout map, and are chock-full of photos.

"Frommer's Italy Day by Day," "Frommer's Ireland Day by Day" and "Frommer's Hawaii Day by Day" are available now, while Costa Rica and Spain are due out in October.

The guides, all under $ 30, include easy-to-use features like what to see if you have a day, three days or a week, and "best-of" lists for lodging, dining and shopping. The Ireland guide, for example, includes a list of favorite moments (taking afternoon tea at the Shelbourne Hotel in Dublin, visiting the Giant's Causeway, and seeing the murals of the Belfast peace wall), along with a list of favorite small towns (Carlingford, Inistioge, Kinsale, Kenmare, Dingle).

Also new from Frommer's is "500 Adrenaline Adventures," providing inspiration for daredevils, geeks and other travelers with a taste for unusual, wacky and heart-racing experiences. Among the ideas listed in the $ 20 paperback: ziplining, wildlife encounters, extreme eating contests, like the famous Coney Island hot dog competition, and the annual Gloucestershire Cheese Rolling Race in England.

DK EYEWITNESS TRAVEL'S BACK ROADS: Road trips are a beloved way to explore America, but DK Eyewitness Travel has launched a new series this spring to inspire road trips in Europe. The "Back Roads" series includes guides to

France, Italy, Great Britain, Ireland and Spain. Each $ 25 paperback describes two dozen "leisurely drives" designed to take anywhere from a day to a week. Tours outlined in the France book, for example, include the Alsace wine route, Obernai to Eguisheim; the Champagne route, Reims to Montagne de Reims, Normandy, from Giverny to Varengeville-sur-Mer; and the Pyrenees, from Collioure to St-Jean-de-Luz.

Other features include mapped itineraries with highlights, detours and activities; "where the locals go" listings of small hotels and restaurants with regional cuisine; a pullout country map; zip codes to make it easy to coordinate the text with a GPS; and practical information on driving conditions, road signs and parking.

LUXURY COLLECTION DESTINATION GUIDES: This set of six paperbacks from The Luxury Collection Hotels & Resorts, a group of more than 70 hotels and resorts in 30 countries, includes guides to India, Italy, the U. S., Spain, Argentina and Greece. The slim paperbacks do not offer the detailed content of traditional travel guides but do have lush photographs, inspirational quotes and a few pages of highlights listing select museums, cultural institutions, shops and restaurants in each destination.

Each guide also includes commentary from celebrity chefs, with Mario Batali providing his thoughts on Italy, including a recipe for tortelloni with sage butter and his recommendations for favorite restaurants: Cibreo and Teatro del Sale in Florence; Al Covo, Da Fiore and Lina d'Ombra in Venice, and Ristorante Matricianella, Roscioli, Antico Forno and Checchino in Rome.

The set of six, packaged in a beautiful oversized box, costs $ 140. The books will be available in Luxury Collection guest rooms, in Assouline Boutiques in Las Vegas, Los Angeles and New York, and online at http://www. luxurycollection. com and other retailers.

THE SMART FAMILY'S PASSPORT: This book from Budget Travel, $ 14. 95, is subtitled "350 Money, Time & Sanity Saving tips." Among the suggestions: Bring powdered iced-tea or fruit-punch packets to theme parks and add them to cups of water to save money on expensive drinks; find out if a membership to your local museum has reciprocal privileges at other institutions where you can get in free when you travel; and make your own picture dictionary. That way, if you don't know a foreign word for bathroom or taxi, you can get help from a local wherever you are just by pulling up the picture of the object on your phone or camera.

http://news. yahoo. com/s/ap _ travel/20100427/ap _ tr _ ge/travel _ by _ the _ book _ new _ travel _ books

Discussion

Discuss the following questions with your class.

1. What do you know of Italy?

2. What factors will you take into account when planning a trip?

3. What do you think of the job as a guide?

4. Which cities attract you most all over the world? What are the reasons?

Unit Ten
Science and Technology

■ **Section A** ■

North Korean Red Star Operating System Details Emerge

The Issue in the News

    North Korea is widely considered to lag behind in its computer technology. Recently, an operating system named Red Star arouses people's concern. Red Star is North Korea's very own Linux-based operating system, featuring a desktop very similar to Windows—but for the red star that replaces the Start button. It first came to light when Mikhail, a Russian blogger living in Pyongyang, picked up a copy for $ 5 near Kim Il-sung University. The install disk apparently features a quote from Kim Jong-il about the importance of an operating system "compatible with Korean traditions," and the system requirements are a Pentium Ⅲ 800MHz with 256MB RAM and 3GB hard drive space (North Korea's version of Minesweeper must take up a lot of room).

The "Red Star" computer operating system has some good and bad points, as all computer operating systems invariably do. On the plus side, it has "good startup music", the Korean folk song "Arirang". And it features world-class security programs designed to keep tabs on who accesses what and to keep outsiders, outside.

On the downside, it features a few knockoff Microsoft programs of ten years ago (word processing, spread sheet, and a few others) and little else. Its lack of programming means that the few North Koreans with clearance to use computers will hardly get much benefit out of the experience. As for web surfing, the Internet is limited to a handful of acceptable sites.

No matter what purpose Red Star is designed for, it is quite obvious that once again North Korea is attempting to prove how self-sufficient they are.

Points to Notice

As you may read, pay attention to the following facets and information mentioned in this piece of news:

● the operating system's emphasis on Internet security and information control

● Red Star components: applicable programme, games, browser etc.

Text

6 April 2010

Details of a home-grown computer operating system developed by North Korea have emerged.

Information about Red Star, as it is known, was made public by a Russian blogger studying in North Korea, who bought the program off the street.

Further analysis by a government institute in neighbouring South Korea said the operating system is aimed at monitoring user activity.

However, very few North Koreans own a computer or have internet access.

Web content is also heavily censored.

It is designed "to control [North Korea's] own information security", a report by South Korea's Science and Technology Policy Institute (STPI)[1] said.

"Due to few applicable programmes available, Red Star will not even be easily distributed in North Korea," it added.

The Russian blogger, identified only as Mikhail, said Red Star could be bought in Pyongyang for around $ 5. He has also posted a series of screenshots on his blog.

Pigeon mail

The operating system represents the determination of North Korea to advance its own computer technology, based on its "Juche" self-reliance philosophy.

The Red Star operating system uses a popular Korean folk song as its start-up music and numbers years using a calendar which starts counting from the birth of state founder Kim Il-sung, making 2010 the 99th year.

It is Linux-based but is heavily influenced by Microsoft with open-source versions of the software giant's Office programmes, including several familiar games.

It runs only in the Korean language and takes 15 minutes to install, reports said.

It has games, an e-mail system known as Pigeon and a Mozilla's Firefox internet browser-which has the North Korean government website as a home page.

The US government has banned the uploading and downloading of open source code to residents of a handful of countries on its sanctions list, which includes North Korea.

The STPI report also said that North Korea has launched a cyber-war unit that targets sites in South Korea and the US.

In July last year South Korea experienced a wave of cyber-attacks which attempted to paralyse a number of websites. US websites including the Pentagon and the White House were also targeted.

Reports suggested that the attacks might have originated in North Korea.

http://news. bbc. co. uk/2/hi/technology/8604912. stm

Online Resources

http://news. bbc. co. uk/2/hi/asia-pacific/8586440. stm

http://news. bbc. co. uk/2/hi/asia-pacific/8579906. stm

http://news. bbc. co. uk/2/hi/asia-pacific/8569001. stm

http://news. bbc. co. uk/2/hi/asia-pacific/8460129. stm

Vocabulary

1.	censor	vt. /vi.	to examine books, films, letters etc to remove anything that is considered offensive, morally harmful, or politically dangerous etc
2.	applicable	adj.	capable of or suitable for being applied
3.	screenshot	n.	an image that shows the contents of a computer display
4.	sanction	n.	[plural] official orders or laws stopping trade, communication etc with another country, as a way of forcing its leaders to make political changes
5.	paralyse	vt.	(paralyze American English) if something paralyses you, it makes you lose the ability to move part or all of your body, or to feel it
6.	pentagon	n.	a flat shape with five sides and five angles(usu. refers to us Ministry of Defence when p is capitalized)

Language Notes

South Korea's Science and Technology Policy Institute (STPI) provides the government with policy alternatives based on research and analysis on key issues in science and technology, assists private industries with strategies for innovation, and disseminates information on science and technology policy, indicators and statistics.

Exercises

 Vocabulary and Expressions

A. Idioms and Expressions

Fill in the blanks with the correct idiom or expression.

aim at: intend or try to do sth. 力求做某事
We must aim at increasing/to increase exports.

due to: caused by sb./sth, because of sb/sth 由于,因为
His successes were largely due to luck.

base on: use sth as grounds, evidence, etc for sth else 基于,以……为依据
The novel is based on historical facts.

1. The television station apologized for the interference, which was _____ bad weather conditions.

2. Direct taxation is usually _____ income.

3. You should always _____ doing your job well.

B. Vocabulary

Fill in the blanks with the words given below. Change the form where necessary.

censor   applicable   screenshot   sanction   paralyse

1. Her legs were partly _____ in the crash.

2. The UN security council may impose economic _____.

3. The offer is only _____ to bookings for double rooms.

4. The information given to the press was carefully _____ by the Ministry of Defence.

✉ Exploring Content

A. Complete the sentences based on the reading text.

1. Further analysis by a government institute in neighbouring South Korea said the operating system _____ .

2. " _____ , Red Star will not even by easily distributed in North Korea," it added.

3. The operating system represents _____
__ , based on its "Juche" self-reliance philosophy.

4. The US government has banned _____
_____ on its sanctions list, which includes North Korea.

5. In July last year South Korea _____
__ which attempted to paralyse a number of websites.

B. Put a check(✓) next to the statements that the writer would agree with.

1. (   ) Information about Red Star, as it is known, was made public by a German blogger studying in North Korea, who bought the program off the street.

2. (   ) However, many North Koreans own a computer or have internet access.

3. (   ) The Red Star operating system uses a popular Korean folk song as its start-up music and numbers years using a calendar which starts counting from the birth of state founder Kim Il-sung, making 2010 the 99th year.

4. (   ) It runs not only in the Korean language and takes 5 minutes to install, reports said. It has games, an e-mail system known as Pigeon and a Mozilla's Firefox internet browser-which has the North Korean government website as a home page.

5. (   ) The STPI report also said that North Korea has launched a cyber-war unit that targets sites in South Korea and the US.

Translation

Translate the following sentences into Chinese.

1. Further analysis by a government institute in neighbouring South Korea said the operating system is aimed at monitoring user activity.

2. The operating system represents the determination of North Korea to advance its own computer technology, based on its "Juche" self-reliance philosophy.

3. The Red Star operating system uses a popular Korean folk song as its start-up music.

4. The US government has banned the uploading and downloading of open source code to residents of a handful of countries on its sanctions list, which includes North Korea.

5. In July last year South Korea experienced a wave of cyber-attacks which attempted to paralyse a number of websites.

 Cloze

Complete the following short passage by choosing proper words from the word bank provided.

maximum designed superficial monitor aimed differ available
obvious impossible prove access proper approximately
tendency date

An operating system __1__ by North Koreans is now available in Pyongyang for about five dollars. This may not seem like a lot of money. Consider, though, the fact that most people in North Korea don't have computer or Internet __2__. There is much speculation flying about as to whether the operating system is designed solely to __3__ every move of the people in that nation. A South Korean government institute has stated unequivocally that the os "is __4__ at monitoring user activity."

The Red Star operating system plays a Korean folk song for the start-up music, and is only __5__ in the Korean language. It reportedly installs in __6__ fifteen minutes.

One detail that strikes me as strange is the way the calendar and dates are set up.

The first ___7___ counted is that of the birth of state founder Kim Il-sung. That means that 2010 is only the 99th year in "history."

The operating system is Linux-based, but you'll find some touches of Microsoft thrown in. There are variations of the Office suite included, as well as several games you'll find familiar.

The email system is called Pigeon... and the browser is Firefox. The home page, however, isn't set to the Mozilla start page. Instead, users logging on to the Internet for the first time will find themselves at the North Korean government website.

While it's ___8___ to tell from these details whether or not the os is designed to spy on (and control) those who use it, it is quite ___9___ that once again North Korea is attempting to ___10___ how self-sufficient they are.

Discussion

Discuss the following questions with your class.

1. What do you know about the country North Korea?
2. How do you think about the relationship between North and South Korea?
3. Both China and North Korean are socialist countries, what is the difference between the two nations?
4. In your opinion, what will happen if every North Korean has easy access to the Internet?

Section B

Mobile TV's Last Frontier: U. S. and Europe

By Kevin J. O'brien

May 30, 2010

BERLIN—When South Korea plays Greece on June 12 in its World Cup soccer opener in Port Elizabeth, South Africa, life will not necessarily grind to a halt back in Seoul.

Many fans will instead follow a live broadcast of the match on their mobile phones. In South Korea, free-to-air mobile TV is a five-year-old fact of life. According to the country's broadcasters, 27 million people—56 percent of the population—watch regularly.

While South Koreans are the world leaders in mobile TV viewing, the technology is also catching on in China, southeast Asia, India, Africa and Latin America, where 80 million people now have cellphones that can receive free, live TV broadcasts.

"There have been a lot of hype cycles with mobile TV technology," said Anna Maxbauer, an analyst at IMS Research in Austin, Texas. "But with recent advances in battery life, and consumer acceptance, there is real potential for widespread viewing."

At least 40 million people are watching live TV this year on mobile phones, Ms. Maxbauer said. Most live in emerging markets where operators, which prefer to sell TV programming for a fee through their wireless networks, do not control the sale of handsets.

Free, on-the-go viewing is common just about everywhere except the United States and Europe, where operator resistance and a maze of conflicting technical standards and program licensing hurdles have kept the technology out of the global mainstream.

But that may be about to change, according to one handset maker.

"This technology has huge potential," said Hankil Yoon, the vice president of product strategy at Samsung, the South Korean electronics maker and U. S. cellphone market leader. "Our experience shows that people like watching TV on mobile phones, even on smaller screens. And they like watching it for free. It is only a matter of time before this goes global. "

In the complex world of wireless communication, free-to-air mobile TV technology is relatively simple. With a tiny receiver chip and telescoping antenna, a mobile phone can receive free digital or analog programming like any other television.

In South Korea, 25 million people watch free digital terrestrial broadcasts on mobile handsets and two million pay to subscribe to satellite programming, according to Korean broadcasters. The typical screen made by Samsung is a three-inch, or 7. 6-centimeter, diagonal. Batteries support three to six hours of viewing. In Korea, free mobile TV broadcasts are interspersed with ads.

"In the markets where people use this, we have found that viewing tends to be pretty high, " said Diana Jovin, a vice president for corporate marketing and business development at Telegent Systems, the leading mobile TV chip maker, which is based in Sunnyvale, California.

Telegent is shipping about 750,000 chips each month to handset makers, most designed for viewing analog broadcasts in markets like Brazil, Peru, Argentina, Russia, Nigeria, Thailand, Egypt and China. Brazil is one of Telegent's biggest markets.

In Rio de Janiero, Marcelo Mendonça Guimarães, a 42-year-old taxi driver, said he watched local and national TV news on his mobile handset through his operator, Claro.

"My analog TV phone gives me the opportunity to watch television news while I'm waiting for a fare, or when I am on a break," Mr. Guimarães said. "I actually have a digital TV in my cab, but I prefer to use the phone. The reception is much better."

Following a favorite team or soap opera on a cellphone may take longer to reach Western markets, where broadcasters and wireless operators have been slow to embrace the technology. In the United States and Europe, where operators tend to control what technology goes into handsets, a major hurdle to free-to-air broadcasting is, ironically, that it is free.

That offers no incentive to operators focused on raising revenue per customer.

"Ask anybody if they want to watch free TV on their phone. Everybody is going to want to say sure," said Jim Oehlerking, the senior director for mobile TV business development at Motorola. "The challenge is getting the mobile media marketplace to the point where content owners, carriers and broadcasters work out a business model."

But with the level of data traffic surging on wireless networks around the world, some operators are beginning to look to free-to-air mobile TV—which operates independently and adds no additional traffic burden on an operator's network—as a way to retain customers.

In April, 12 broadcasters and television content owners in the United States, including Fox, NBC, Gannett Broadcasting, Hearst and Cox Media, formed a joint venture to pool their broadcasting spectrum and eventually deliver mobile TV to 150 million people.

"We are excited about building a platform that makes mobile television universally available and economically viable," Jack Abernethy, the chief executive of Fox Television Stations, said at the time of the announcement. "This venture is the first step in forging cross-industry and company partnerships to deliver content to consumers."

The U. S. effort is in its initial stages, and no deadlines have been set for adoption.

Samsung, which includes mobile TV chips as standard technology in its high-end smartphones in South Korea, is making a handset for Sprint that works on the U. S. mobile broadcast standard, ATSC-M/H. Samsung also makes a DVB-H phone for Europe, two that work on Latin America's ISDB-T standard and an analog handset for Southeast Asia.

On May 24, Sprint and nine broadcasters in the Washington-Baltimore area began a four-month trial that will broadcast programming to mobile phones, netbook computers and portable DVD players made by Samsung, LG Electronics and Dell.

Dave Lougee, the president of Gannett Broadcasting, said the organizers of the trial, a group of 900 U. S. television stations called the Open Mobile Video Coalition, were hopeful consumers would take to the technology.

The trial is being supported by every facet of the U. S. television industry, including content owners, broadcasters, broadcast equipment makers and advertisers, represented by the Television Bureau of Advertisers and The Ad Council.

"We are looking forward to hearing how consumers use the technology," Mr. Lougee said in announcing the trial.

If South Korea is a guide, U. S. consumers will use it just as much, if the price is right.

http://www. nytimes. com/2010/05/31/technology/31mobiletv. html? pagewanted = 2&ref = technology

Vocabulary

Match each word to its definition.

1. grind   (   )   a. of, relating to, or being a mechanism in which data is represented by continuously variable physical quantities

2. hype   (   )   b. relating to the Earth rather than to the moon or other

3. mince   (   )   c. to cut food, especially raw meat, into very small pieces by putting it through a machine

4. hurdle   (   )   d. able to continue to live or to develop into a living thing

5. antenna   (   )   e. joining two vertices of a rectilinear figure that are nonadjacent or two vertices of a polyhedral figure that are not in the same face

6. analog   (   )   f. attempts to make people think something is good or important by talking about it a lot on television, the radio etc-used to show disapproval

7. terrestrial   (   )   g. a complete range of opinions, people, situations etc, going from one extreme to its opposite

8. diagonal   (   )   h. a complicated and confusing arrangement of streets, roads etc

9. intersperse   (   )   i. a problem or difficulty that you must deal with before you can achieve something

10. spectrum   (   )   j. to place something at intervals in or among

11. viable   (   )   k. one of two long thin parts on an insect's head, that it uses to feel things

Discussion

Discuss the following questions with your class.

1. What are the advantages of mobile TV?

2. Do you think watching TV on mobile phones will go global?

3. In your opinion, what are the culture symbols of South Korea?

4. According to you, what are the most important functions of cell phone?

Section C

White-hot Energy

From *The Economist* online

Apr 19th 2010

New power sources could be made using magnesium

STORING energy is one of the biggest obstacles to the widespread adoption of alternative sources of power. Batteries can be bulky and slow to charge. Hydrogen, which can be made electrolytically from water and used to power fuel cells, is difficult to handle. But there may be an alternative: magnesium. As school chemistry lessons show, metallic magnesium is highly reactive and stores a lot of energy. Even a small amount of magnesium ribbon burns in a flame with a satisfying white heat. Researchers are now devising ways to extract energy from magnesium in a more controlled fashion.

Engineers at MagPower in White Rock, British Columbia, for example, have developed a metal-air cell that uses water and ambient air to react with a magnesium fuel supply, in the form of a metal anode, to generate electricity. Doron Aurbach at Bar-Ilan University, Israel, has created a magnesium-based version of the lithium-ion rechargeable cell, a type of battery known for its long life and stability. It would be ideal for storing electricity from renewable sources, says Dr Aurbach. And Andrew Kindler at the California Institute of Technology in Pasadena is developing a way for cars to generate hydrogen on board by reacting magnesium fuel with steam. The reaction produces a pure form of hydrogen suitable for fuel cells, leaving behind only magnesium oxide, a relatively benign material, as a by-product.

But there is, of course, a catch. Although magnesium is abundant, its production is neither cheap nor clean, says Takashi Yabe of the Tokyo Institute of Technology. Various industrial methods are used to extract magnesium, ranging from an electrolytic process to a high temperature method called the Pidgeon process, but the energy cost is high. Producing a single kilogram of magnesium requires 10kg of coal, says Dr Yabe.

To change this, he is developing a process using only renewable energy. Dr Yabe's solution is to use concentrated solar energy to power a laser, which is used to heat and ultimately burn magnesium oxide extracted from seawater—where, he says, there is enough magnesium to meet the world's energy needs for the next 300,000 years. A solar-pumped laser is necessary, he says, because concentrated solar energy alone would not be enough to generate the 3,700℃ temperatures required. Dr Yabe calls his approach the Magnesium Injection Cycle.

The pure magnesium can then be used as a fuel (its energy density is about ten times that of hydrogen). When the magnesium is mixed with water, it produces heat, boiling the water to produce steam, which can then drive a turbine and do useful work. The reaction also produces hydrogen, which can be burned to produce even more energy. The byproducts are water and magnesium oxide, which can then be converted back into magnesium using the solar laser.

The trouble is that concentrated solar collectors tend to be huge and costly, and solar-pumped lasers are normally very low powered. Dr Yabe's trick is to use relatively small Fresnel lenses—transparent and relatively thin planar lenses made up of concentric rings of prisms. These are commonly found in lighthouses to magnify light in a way that would normally require a much larger, thicker lens. His other trick is to boost the output power of the lasing material, neodymium-doped yttrium aluminum garnet. It normally only absorbs about 7% of the energy from sunlight, but when doped with chromium this figure increases to more than 67%.

Dr Yabe has built a demonstration plant at Chitose, Japan, in partnership with Mitsubishi. It is capable of producing 80 watts of power from the laser, enough to cut steel and extract 70% of the magnesium in seawater. The process will, says Dr Yabe, become commercially viable when the laser power reaches 400 watts, which could happen later this year. "As a starting point we are planning to use 300 lasers to produce 50 tonnes of magnesium per year," he says. After that, it is just a small matter of convincing the world to start thinking about a magnesium economy instead of hydrogen one, he adds.

http://www. economist. com/science-technology/technology-monitor/displayStory. cfm? story _ id =15939644

Discussion

Discuss the following questions with your class.

1. Do you know where magnesium can be applied?

2. What kind of food is rich in magnesium?

3. Can you introduce some ways to access energy?

4. Do you think extracting energy from magnesium will become a popular way?

Keys

Unit One

Section A

Vocabulary and Expressions

A. 1. have in mind　2. has taken on　3. be nuts about

B. 1. embodiment　2. gargantuan　3. wizardry　4. rebut　5. mangled　6. incursions

7. bombard　8. Aquatic　9. dynamism　10. rollercoaster

Exploring Content

A. 1. T　2. F　3. T　4. F　5. F

B. 1. symbolise　2. startling　3. reveal　4. vogue　5. giant

Translation

1. 东伦敦将拥有这个国家最大、最具野心的艺术品:让人惊叹的看起来像一个被损坏的过山车似的红色塔形建筑。

2. 约翰逊先生说大伦敦政府将承担310万英镑的花费,剩余的则全部由米塔尔先生负责。

3. 他说:"我很清楚,会有人说我们是傻瓜,我们愚蠢到在经济极端衰退的情况下修建英国有史以来最大的公共艺术设施。"

4. 它是以拉克西米·米塔尔所拥有的钢铁公司命名的,米塔尔是英国最富有的人,他将支付大部分费用。

5. 电梯和一个行人道每小时可将800人送达顶部,那里将建有一个餐厅和一个观景台。

Cloze

1. collision　2. Monument　3. unveiled　4. instantly　5. described　6. viewing

7. offered　8. terribly　9. entire　10. structure

Section B

Vocabulary

1—d 2—a 3—b 4—g 5—c 6—e 7—f

Unit Two

Section A

Vocabulary and Expressions

A. 1. name after 2. specialize in 3. devotes...to

B. 1. strain 2. abruptly 3. demise 4. startup 5. sartorial 6. lengthy 7. boutique

   8. traction

Exploring Content

A. 1. where both women were born and raised 2. financial management and operations

   3. she still sported Maria Pinto every now and then 4. whose New York location will soon be closing its doors 5. I was discovering Michelle Obama's style influence

B. 2. ✓ 3. 4. ✓ 5. ✓

Translation

1. 时尚与政治都是季节性的、不可预知的。

2. 平托女士承认在建设自己的品牌之初就在财务管理和运作方面犯了一些错误。

3. 奥巴马夫人成为第一夫人之后,风格多变。

4. 即使是(奥巴马夫人)这样高调的支持这一品牌,其昂贵的价格还是不能将其从经济衰退的现实中解救出来。

5. 平托女士在总结前几个月的情况时说:"的确,这使人心碎悲伤,但所幸的是,我的创造力将一直伴随我前行。"

Cloze

1. choice 2. discovered 3. craft 4. creative 5. favorite 6. earnings 7. appear

8. editor 9. wore 10. interviewed

Section B

1—d 2—f 3—e 4—a 5—b 6—c 7—j 8—g 9—h 10—i

Unit Three

Section A

Vocabulary and Expressions

A. 1. for himself 2. in place 3. for himself

B. 1. hastily 2. jeopardize 3. eclipsed 4. unprecedented 5. mitigate 6. legitimate
 7. sprawling 8. stemmed

Exploring Content

A. 1. Lamar McKay 2. Barack Obama 3. Barack Obama 4. Bobby Jindal
 5. Tony Hayward 6. Ken Salazar

B. 1. potentially 2. temporary 3. threaten 4. executive 5. priority

Translation

1. 总统奥巴马在路易斯安那州发言时提到,美国政府会尽一切可能清理泄漏的石油,并指出英国石油公司应对此次事件负责并作出赔偿。

2. 奥巴马指出目前关注点要投放在防止墨西哥湾海岸进一步遭破坏上。

3. 英国石油公司称出台防止石油泄漏的临时性措施至少要一周时间。

4. 他在威尼斯发言时说:"我们正在应对一次巨大的、有可能是前所未见的环境灾难。"

5. 密西西比州、亚拉巴马州和佛罗里达州都宣布进入紧急状态,并考虑采取法律手段。

Cloze

1. anticipated 2. warn 3. number 4. jeopardy 5. flock 6. migration 7. either
 8. shelter 9. casualties 10. wildlife

Section B

Vocabulary

1—c 2—e 3—a 4—f 5—b 6—h 7—d 8—g

Unit Four

Section A

Vocabulary and Expressions

A. 1. cheered on 2. spurred on 3. by far 4. kick off

B. 1. initiative   2. objective   3. mobilize   4. humanity   5. harness   6. Emission

7. projector   8. highlight   9. landmark

Exploring Content

A. 1. major landmark; triumph

2. an opportunity on the playing field of life

3. the opportunities; boost social, economic and environmental development

4. harness the power of sport to promote children's rights

5. child abuse; exploitation; child sex tourism; trafficking

B. 1. tournament   2. critical   3. discrimination   4. boost   5. campaign

Translation

1. 世界杯首次在非洲国家举行,联合国期望借此影响来实现诸多目标:从保证素质教育和一个干净的环境到减少饥饿和疾病。

2. 联合国秘书长潘基文参加了今天在约翰内斯堡举行的世界杯开幕仪式和首场比赛,他认为世界杯对非洲人民而言是个里程碑,也是人道主义的胜利。

3. 联合国秘书长潘基文和整个联合国正利用此次世界杯来推动联合国千年发展目标的实现,即世界各国领导人承诺在 2015 年之前实现的八个目标。

4. 当我们为足球场上的球队欢呼时,请记住:联合国千年发展目标不是光看不动就能实现的。

5. 体育有一种独特的力量能吸引人们,调动人们和鼓舞人们,同时也是目前最受年轻人喜爱的一项活动。

Cloze

1. influential   2. win   3. Brazilian   4. confident   5. crowns   6. objective   7. prepare

8. shape   9. throughout   10. fundamental

Section B

Vocabulary

1—i   2—d   3—g   4—j   5—c   6—h   7—k   8—b   9—f   10—a   11—l   12—e

Unit Five

Section A

Vocabulary and Expressions

A. 1. is related to   2. suffer from   3. on average

B. 1. digestive 2. categories 3. symptoms 4. confirm 5. residential 6. prevalent

7. infectious 8. diminished 9. pollutant 10. disorder

Exploring Content

A. 1. The annual rates of 15 out of 24 major physical diseases were also significantly lower among those living closer to green spaces.

2. For depression the rates were 32 per 1 000 for the people in the more built up areas and 24 per 1 000 for those in the greener areas.

3. The researchers also showed that this relation was strongest for children younger than 12.

4. They were 21% less likely to suffer from depression in the greener areas.

5. Two unexpected findings were that the greener spaces did not show benefits for high blood pressure and that the relation appeared stronger for people aged 46 to 65 than for the elderly.

B. 1. impact 2. noticeable 3. contain 4. costly 5. diminish

Translation

1. 居住在绿地附近的人患 24 种主要身体疾病中的 15 种病的几率明显较低。

2. 当绿化在居住地一千米半径之内时它对大多数疾病的健康益处才能显现出来。

3. 研究者们还表示这种关联在 12 岁以下的儿童身上表现最为突出。

4. 在绿化较好的区域他们患抑郁症的几率就会降低 21%。

5. 研究者们认为绿地可以帮助人们从压力中恢复过来并提供了更多社交机会。

Cloze

1. protect 2. boosting 3. Across 4. generally 5. extent 6. unhealthy 7. regardless

8. analysed 9. difference 10. fewest

Section B

1—c 2—e 3—a 4—b 5—f 6—i 7—d 8—k 9—l 10—g 11—h 12—m

13—j

Unit Six

Section A

Vocabulary and Expressions

A. 1. put together 2. count on 3. dried up

B. 1. default 2. dampened 3. woes 4. predecessor 5. currency 6. Aggregate

7. quell 8. predictions 9. stability 10. exceeded

Exploring Content

A. 1. calm fears over the debt problems 2. that normally strong currency (Euro)

3. 3 percent of its gross domestic product 4. deficit reduction 5. make public predictions

B. 1—e 2—c 3—d 4—a 5—b

Translation

1. 此次希腊债务危机对美国人来讲似乎有点遥远,但是专家认为它可能会影响美国以及全球金融业的恢复。

2. 包括法国总统尼古拉斯·萨科奇和德国总理安吉拉·默克尔在内的欧洲最高领导人与希腊总理乔治·帕潘德里欧会面,商讨未来几年希腊降低财政赤字的计划。

3. 由于希腊债务危机的蔓延,欧元兑美元不断贬值,从去年十一月份平均1欧元兑1.49美元降到本周三1欧元兑1.38美元。

4. 如果欧元兑美元贬值,也就意味着美国商品对欧洲人来说更贵了,那么购买者就会减少。

5. 一位公司发言人说道,现在来判定欧洲债务危机是否会影响卡特彼勒的业务还为时尚早。

Cloze

1. worst 2. setback 3. comparatively 4. counterparts 5. European 6. preparing

7. buying 8. anxieties 9. fallen 10. remain

Section B

Vocabulary

1—e 2—d 3—f 4—a 5—b 6—h 7—c 8—j 9—g 10—i 11—o 12—p

13—k 14—q 15—l 16—m 17—r 18—n

Unit Seven

Section A

Vocabulary and Expressions

A. 1. in total 2. a spate of 3. a range of

B. 1. standard 2. suicide 3. previously 4. overtook 5. sweatshop 6. controversial

7. spate 8. comment 9. range 10. spotlights

Exploring Content

A. 1. Foxconn is not a sweatshop 2. it will give its assembly line workers a 30% pay rise

3. who earn 900 yuan (￡90) per month at entry-level 4. allow them to have more leisure

time, which is good for their health 5. become the world's largest technology company by

market value

B. 5. ✓ 6. ✓

Translation

1. 富士康今年总共已有13起自杀和企图自杀事件发生。

2. 富士康新进员工每月的基本薪资是900元(90英镑),公司之前曾说过要给他们加
   薪20%。

3. 富士康员工跳楼事件引起了人们对工厂工作条件的关注。富士康的员工多数来自中国
   的农村地区,他们每周工作6天,每天工作12小时。

4. 上周,苹果公司超过微软成为全球市值最大的科技公司。

5. 他(苹果总裁乔布斯)还称苹果拒绝在iPhones和iPads上使用Adobe Flash动画和视频
   技术,这一备受争议的举动是一个技术决定。

Cloze

1. devices 2. commit 3. survived 4. twisted 5. allegedly 6. radical 7. calm

8. clumsy 9. blocking 10. trigger

Section B

1—b 2—c 3—a 4—f 5—d 6—e 7—h 8—i 9—g 10—j

Unit Eight

Section A

Vocabulary and Expressions

A. 1. ruled out 2. stamp out 3. forged ahead

B. 1. humiliating 2. sleaze 3. battered 4. emissions 5. stagnation 6. confirmed

7. implored 8. alliance 9. prosperity 10. advocating

Exploring Content

A. 1. ruling Democrats after Yukio Hatoyama's resignation over economy and US airbase

  2. it confronts economic stagnation, mounting public debt and regional instability

  3. ending more than 50 years of almost uninterrupted rule by the conservative Liberal Democratic party

  4. in the face of the tough political situation and fight as a united force

  5. pressured Japan's central bank to take a more active role in fighting deflation

B. 1. ✓ 3. ✓

Translation

1. 由于日本当前面临着经济停滞、公共债务不断增加和地区不稳定的问题,菅直人当选后迅速做出重建日本的承诺。

2. 还有几周就会迎来关键的参议院选举,菅直人恳请党内成员接触那些在去年8月以绝对多数票把他们选出来的选民。

3. 日本要以日美同盟为外交基轴,同时还必须要努力促进亚洲地区的繁荣。

4. 菅直人维持鸠山的承诺,即在未来10年日本将温室气体排放量较1990年水准减少25%。

5. 菅直人当选首相有助于扭转日元进一步疲软趋势,但他正考虑增加消费税,这将对股票市场产生负面影响。

Cloze

1. revitalise 2. ranging 3. address 4. sworn 5. continuity 6. former 7. succeed

8. stagnation 9. appointed 10. enthusiastic

Section B

1—g 2—a 3—d 4—f 5—c 6—e 7—b 8—i 9—j 10—h

Unit Nine

Section A

Vocabulary and Expressions

A. 1. take on 2. lingers over 3. slipped into

B. 1. evoked 2. off-limits 3. tribute 4. quipped 5. fleeing 6. elastic 7. enticing

8. facsimile   9. trickle   10. exile   11. aerial   12. replica

Exploring Content

A. 1. T   2. F   3. T   4. F   5. F

B. 1. steep   2. exclusively   3. confused   4. elicit   5. nostalgia

Translation

1. 不断有部分美国游客继续通过来自坎昆和拿骚的航班进入哈瓦那,悄悄验证奥巴马政权关于在海外风俗问讯处"不问不答"有关古巴旅游政策的事实。

2. 主办方期待三天会有三万游客来参观古巴的艺术、音乐、饮食而且在古巴购物。

3. "说起哈瓦那,有时我都不能记得他到底是我自己的记忆,还是有人告诉过我,甚或我在某本画册里看过。"

4. 像在前些年,一些老夫妇们会盯着1953年时的哈瓦那的巨幅照片看上半天,给他们的孩子和孙子们指他们以前的家(有些废弃了,有些被占领了)。

5. 而且很确定的是依然是以50年代三分钱的价格就可以喝到古巴咖啡。

Cloze

1. alliance   2. soared   3. devoted   4. drop   5. tropical   6. due   7. collapse   8. back

9. Tourism   10. available

Section B

Vocabulary

1—c   2—e   3—g   4—h   5—i   6—b   7—d   8—a   9—f

Unit Ten

Section A

Vocabulary

A. 1. due to   2. based on   3. aim at

B. 1. paralysed   2. sanctions   3. applicable   4. censored

Exploring Content

A. 1. is aimed at monitoring user activity   2. Due to few applicable programmes available   3. the determination of North Korea to advance its own computer technology   4. the uploading and downloading of open source code to residents of a handful of countries

    5．experienced a wave of cyber-attacks

B．3. ✓　5. ✓

Translation

    1．韩国一家政府机构所作的进一步分析认为红星操作系统旨在监控用户活动。

    2．红星操作系统表明朝鲜基于自主的主体思想推动本国电脑技术向前发展的决心。

    3．红星操作系统使用一首非常流行的朝鲜民歌作为开机音乐。

    4．美国政府已经禁止包括朝鲜在内的制裁名单上的国家居民上传和下载开放源编码。

    5．去年 7 月,韩国遭遇了一波企图使他们许多网站瘫痪的网络袭击。

Cloze

    1．designed　2．access　3．monitor　4．aimed　5．available　6．approximately　7．date

    8．impossible　9．obvious　10．prove

Section B

Vocabulary

    1—c　2—f　3—h　4—i　5—k　6—a　7—b　8—e　9—j　10—g　11—d